Comfort to the Enemy
and other
Carl Webster Tales

Also by Elmore Leonard

Fiction

Road Dogs

Up in Honey's Room

The Hot Kid

The Complete Western
Stories of Elmore Leonard

Mr Paradise

When the Women Come Out To
Dance

Tishomingo Blues

Pagan Babies

Be Cool

The Tonto Woman & Other
Western Stories

Cuba Libre

Out of Sight

Riding the Rap

Pronto

Rum Punch

Maximum Bob

Get Shorty

Killshot

Freaky Deaky

Touch

Bandits

Glitz

LaBrava

Stick

Cat Chaser

Split Images

City Primeval

Gold Coast

Gunsights

The Switch

The Hunted

Unknown Man No. 89

Swag

Fifty-two Pickup

Mr. Majestyk

Forty Lashes Less One

Valdez Is Coming

The Moonshine War

The Big Bounce

Hombre

Last Stand at Saber River

Escape from Five Shadows

The Law at Randado

The Bounty Hunters

Non-fiction

Elmore Leonard's 10 Rules of Writing

COMFORT TO THE ENEMY

AND OTHER
CARL WEBSTER TALES

ELMORE LEONARD

Weidenfeld & Nicolson

LONDON

First published in Great Britain in 2009
by Weidenfeld & Nicolson

An imprint of The Orion Publishing Group Ltd
Orion House, 5 Upper Saint Martin's Lane
London WC2H 9EA
An Hachette UK Company

10 9 8 7 6 5 4 3 2 1

A CIP catalogue record for this book is
available from the British Library.

ISBN (Hardback) 978 0 297 85668 9
ISBN (Export Trade Paperback) 978 0 297 85669 6

Typeset by Input Data Services Ltd, Bridgwater, Somerset

Printed and bound in Great Britain by Clays Ltd, St Ives plc

The Orion Publishing Group's policy is to use papers that are natural, renewable
and recyclable products and made from wood grown in sustainable forests.
The logging and manufacturing processes are expected to conform to the
environmental regulations of the country of origin.

www.orionbooks.co.uk

For Gregg Sutter, always there

Showdown at Checotah

Elmore Leonard

How Carlos Webster changed his name to Carl
and became a famous Oklahoma lawman

C arlos Webster was 15 years old the time he witnessed the robbery and murder at Deering's drugstore. It was in the summer of 1921. He told Bud Maddox, the Okmulgee chief of police, he had driven a load of cows up to the yard at Tulsa and by the time he got back it was dark. He said he left the stock trailer across the street from Deering's and went inside to get an ice cream cone. When he identified one of the robbers as Frank Miller, Bud Maddox said, 'Son, Frank Miller robs banks, he don't bother with drugstores no more.'

Carlos had been raised on hard work and respect for his elders. He said, 'I could be wrong,' knowing he wasn't.

They brought him over to police headquarters in the court-house to look at photos. He pointed to Frank Miller staring at him from a $500 wanted bulletin and picked the other one, Jim Ray Monks, from mug shots. Bud Maddox said, 'You're positive, huh?' and asked Carlos which one was it shot the Indian. Meaning Junior Harjo, with the tribal police, who'd walked in not knowing the store was being robbed.

'Was Frank Miller shot him,' Carlos said, 'with a .45 Colt.'

'You sure it was a Colt?'

'Navy issue, like my dad's.'

'I'm teasing,' Bud Maddox said. He and Carlos's dad Virgil Webster were buddies, both having fought in the Spanish-American War and for a number of years were the local heroes; but now doughboys were back from France telling about the Great War over there.

'If you like to know what I think happened,' Carlos said, 'Frank Miller only came in for a pack of smokes.'

Bud Maddox stopped him. 'Tell it from the time you got there.'

'Okay, well, the reason was to get an ice cream cone. Mr Deering was in back doing prescriptions – he looked out of that little window and told me to help myself. So I went over to the soda fountain and scooped up a double dip of peach on a sugar cone and went up to the cigar counter and left a nickel by the cash register. That's where I was when I see these two men come in wearing suits and hats I thought at first were salesmen. Mr Deering calls to me to wait on them as I know the store pretty well. Frank Miller comes up to the counter—'

'You knew right away who he was?'

'Once he was close, yes sir, from pictures of him in the paper. He said to give him a deck of Luckies. I did and he picks up the nickel I'd left by the register? Hands it to me and says, "This ought to cover it".'

'You tell him it was yours?'

'No sir.'

'Or a pack of Luckies was fifteen cents?'

'I didn't argue with him. But see, I think that's when he got the idea of robbing the store, the cash register sitting there, nobody around but me holding my ice cream cone. Mr Deering never came out from the back. The other one, Jim Ray Monks? He wanted a tube of Unguentine, he said for a heat rash was bothering him, under his arms. I got it for him and he didn't pay either. Then Frank Miller says, "Let's see what you have in the register." I told him I didn't know how to open it as I didn't work there. He leans over the counter and points to a key – a man who knows his cash registers – and says, "That one right there. Hit it and she'll open for you." I press the key – Mr Deering must've heard it ring open, he calls from the back of the store, "Carlos, you able to help them out?" Frank Miller raised his voice saying, "Carlos is doing fine," using my name. He told me to take out the scrip but leave the change.'

'How much did he get?'

'No more'n fifty dollars,' Carlos said. He took his time thinking about what happened right after, starting with Frank Miller looking at his ice cream cone. Carlos saw it as personal, something between him and Miller, so he skipped over it, telling Bud Maddox: 'I put the money on the counter for him, mostly singles. I look up—'

'Junior Harjo walks in,' Bud Maddox said, 'a robbery in progress?'

'Yes sir, but Junior doesn't know it. Frank Miller's at the counter with his back to him. Jim Ray Monks is over at the soda fountain getting into the ice cream. Neither of them had their guns out, so I doubt Junior saw it as a robbery. But Mr Deering sees Junior and calls out he's got his mother's medicine. Then says for all of us to hear, "She tells me they got you raiding stills, looking for moonshine". He said something about setting a jar aside for him and that's all I heard. Now the guns are coming out, Frank Miller's Colt from inside his suit . . . I guess all he had to see was Junior's badge and his sidearm, that was enough. Frank Miller shot him. He'd know with that Colt one round would do the job, but he stepped up and shot Junior again, lying on the floor.'

There was a silence.

'I'm trying to recall,' Bud Maddox said, 'how many Frank Miller's killed. I believe six, half of 'em police officers.'

'Seven,' Carlos said, 'you count the bank hostage had to stand on his running board. Fell off and broke her neck?'

I just read the report on that one,' Bud Maddox said. 'Was a Dodge Touring, same as Black Jack Pershing's staff car over in France.'

'They drove away from the drugstore in a LaSalle,' Carlos said, and gave Bud Maddox the license number.

Here was the part Carlos saw as personal and had skipped over, beginning with Frank Miller looking at his ice cream cone.

Then asking, 'What is that, peach?' Carlos said it was and Frank Miller reached out his hand saying, 'Lemme have a bite there,' and took the cone to hold it away from him as it was starting to drip. He bent over to lick it a couple of times before putting his mouth around a big bite he took from the top dip. He said, 'Mmm, that's good,' with a trace of peach ice cream along the edge of his mustache. Frank Miller stared at Carlos then like he was studying his features and began licking the cone again. He said, 'Carlos, huh?' cocking his head to one side. 'You got the dark hair, but you don't look like any Carlos to me. What's your other name?'

'Carlos Huntington Webster, that's all of 'em.'

'It's a lot of name for a boy,' Frank Miller said. 'So you're part greaser on your mama's side, huh? What's she, Mex?'

Carlos hesitated before saying, 'Cuban. I was named for her dad.'

'Cuban's the same as Mex,' Frank Miller said. 'You got greaser blood in you, boy, even if it don't show much. You come off lucky there.' He licked the cone again, holding it with the tips of his fingers, the little finger sticking out in a dainty kind of way.

Carlos, 15 years old but as tall as this man with the ice cream on his mustache, wanted to call him a dirty name and hit him in the mouth as hard as he could, then go over the counter and bulldog him to the floor, the way he'd put a bull calf down to brand and cut off its balls. Fifteen years old but he wasn't stupid. He held on while his heart beat against his chest. He felt the need to stand up to this man, saying finally, 'My dad was on the battleship Maine when she was blown up in Havana Harbor, February 15, 1898. He survived and fought the dons with Huntington's Marines in that war in Cuba and met my mother, Graciaplena. When the war was over he went back and brought her to Oklahoma when it was still Indian Territory. She died having me, so I never knew her. I never met my dad's mother, either. She's part Northern Cheyenne, lives on a reservation out at Lame Deer, Montana,' saying it in a voice that was slow and calm compared to what he felt inside. Saying, 'What I want to ask you – if having Indian blood *too* makes me something else besides a greaser.' Saying it in Frank Miller's face, causing this man with ice cream on his mustache to squint at him.

'For one thing,' Frank Miller said, 'the Indian blood makes you and your daddy breeds, him more'n you.' He kept staring at Carlos as he raised the cone, his little finger sticking out, Carlos thinking to lick it again, but what he did was toss the cone over his shoulder, not looking or caring where it would land.

It hit the floor in front of Junior Harjo, just then walking in, badge on his tan shirt, revolver on his hip, and Carlos saw the situation turning around. He felt the excitement of these moments but with some relief, too. It picked him up and gave him the nerve to say to Frank Miller, 'Now you're gonna have to clean up your mess.' Except Junior wasn't pulling his .38, he was looking at the ice cream on the linoleum and Mr Deering was calling to him about his mother's medicine and about raiding stills and Frank Miller was turning from the counter with the Colt in his hand, firing, shooting Junior Harjo and stepping closer to shoot him again.

There was no sign of Mr Deering. Jim Ray Monks came over to have a look at Junior. Frank Miller laid his Colt on the glass counter, picked up the cash in both hands and shoved the bills into his coat pockets before looking at Carlos again.

'You said something to me. Geronimo come in and you said something sounded smart aleck.'

Carlos said, 'What'd you kill him for?' still looking at Junior on the floor.

'I want to know what you said to me.'

Frank Miller waited.

Carlos looked up, rubbing the back of his hand across his mouth. 'I said, now you'll have to clean up your mess. The ice cream on the floor.'

'That's all?'

'It's what I said.'

Frank Miller kept looking at him. 'You had a gun you'd of shot me, huh? Calling you a greaser. Hell, it's a law of nature, you got any of that blood in you you're a greaser. I can't help it, it's how it is. Being a breed on top of it – I don't know if that's called anything or not. But you could pass if you want, you look enough white. Hell, call yourself Carl, I won't tell on you.'

Carlos and his dad lived in a big new house Virgil said was a California bungalow, off the road and into the pecan trees, a house that was all porch across the front and windows in the steep slant of the roof, a house built last year with oil money – those derricks pumping away on a back section of the property. The rest of it was graze and over a thousand acres of pecan trees, Virgil's pride, land gathered over twenty years since coming home from Cuba. He could let the trees go and live high off his oil checks, never work again as long as he lived. Nothing doing – harvest time Virgil was out with his crew shaking pecan trees. He had Carlos seeing to the cows, a hundred or so head of cross-Brahmas at a time, feeding till the day they were shipped to market.

When Carlos got back from a haul, Virgil would be sitting on the porch with a bottle of Mexican beer. Prohibition was no bother, Virgil had a steady supply of beer, tequila and mescal brought up through Texas by the oil people, part of the deal.

The night he witnessed the robbery and murder Carlos sat with his old dad and told him the whole story, including what he'd left out of his account to Bud Maddox, even telling about the ice cream on Frank Miller's mustache. Carlos was anxious to know if his dad thought he might've caused Junior Harjo to get shot. 'I don't see how,' Virgil said, 'from what you told me. I don't know why you'd even think of it, other than you were right there and what you're wondering is if you could've prevented him from getting shot.'

Virgil Webster was 46 years old, a widower since Graciaplena died in ought-six, giving him Carlos and requiring Virgil to look for a woman to nurse the child. He found Narcissa Raincrow, 16, a pretty little Creek girl, daughter of Johnson Raincrow, deceased, an outlaw so threatening, peace officers shot him while he was asleep. Narcissa had lost her own child giving birth, wasn't married, and Virgil hired her as a wetnurse. By the time little Carlos had lost interest in her breasts, Virgil had acquired an appreciation. It wasn't long after Narcissa became their house-keeper she was sleeping in Virgil's bed. She cooked good, put on some weight, but was still pretty, listened to Virgil's stories and laughed when she was supposed to. Carlos loved her, had fun talking to her about Indian ways, and her murderous dad, but never called her anything but Narcissa. Carlos liked the idea of being part Cuban; he saw himself wearing a panama hat when he was older.

He said to his dad that night on the dark porch, 'Are you thinking I should've done something?'

'Like what?'

'Yell at Junior it's a robbery? No, I had to say something smart to Frank Miller. I was mad and wanted to get back at him somehow.'

'For taking your ice cream cone?'

'For what he said.'

'What part was it provoked you?'

'What *part*? What he said about being a greaser.'

'You or your mama?'

'Both. And calling me and you breeds.'

Virgil said, 'You let that bozo get to you? Probably can't read nor write, the reason he has to rob banks. Jesus Christ, get some sense.' He swigged his Mexican beer and said, 'I know what you mean though, how you felt.'

'What would you have done?'

'Same as you, nothing,' Virgil said. 'But if you're talking about in my time, when I was still a marine? I'd of shoved the ice cream cone up his goddamn nose.'

Three days later, sheriff's deputies spotted the LaSalle in the backyard of a farmhouse near Checotah, the house belonging to a woman by the name of Faye Harris. Her former husband, Olin 'Skeet' Harris, deceased, shot dead in a gun battle with US marshals, had at one time been a member of the Frank Miller Gang. The deputies waited for marshals to arrive, as apprehending armed fugitives was their specialty. The marshals slipped into the house at first light, fed the dog, tiptoed into Faye's bedroom and got the drop on Frank Miller before he could dig his Colt from under the pillow.

Jim Ray Monks went out a window, started across the barn lot and caught a load of double-ought that put him down. The two were brought to Okmulgee and locked up to await trial.

Carlos said to his dad, 'Boy, those marshals know their stuff, don't they? Armed killer – they shove a gun in his ear and yank him out of bed.'

He was certain he'd be called to testify and was anxious, couldn't wait. He told his dad he intended to look directly at Frank Miller as he described the cold-blooded killing. Virgil advised him not to say any more than he had to. Carlos said he wondered if he should mention the ice cream on Frank Miller's mustache.

'Why would you want to?' Virgil said.

'Show I didn't miss anything.'

'You know how many times the other night,' Virgil said, 'you told me about the ice cream on his mustache? I'm thinking three or four times.'

'You had to see it. Here's this Frank Miller everybody's scared of, doesn't know enough to wipe his mouth.'

'I'd forget that,' Virgil said. 'He shot a lawman in cold blood. That's all you need to remember about him.'

A month passed and then another, Carlos becoming fidgety. Virgil found out why it was taking so long, came home to Narcissa putting supper on the table, Carlos sitting there, and told them the delay was caused by other counties wanting to get their hands on Frank Miller. So the matter was given to a district court judge to rule on, each county laying out its case, sounding like they'd make a show out of trying him. 'His Honor got our prosecutor to offer Frank Miller a deal,' Virgil said. 'Plead guilty to murder in the second degree, the motive self-defense, as the victim was armed, and give him ten to fifty years. That would be the end of it, no trial needed. In other words, your Frank Miller will get sent to McAlester and be out in five years.'

'There was nothing self-defense about it,' Carlos said. 'Junior wasn't even looking at him when he got shot.' Carlos sounding like he was in pain.

'You don't know the system,' Virgil said. 'The deal worked 'cause Junior's Creek, or else Cherokee. He was a white man, Frank Miller'd be doing twenty-five to life.'

Another event of note took place that same year, 1921, toward the end of October and late in the afternoon, dusk settling in the orchards. Carlos shot and killed a cattle thief by the name of Wally Tarwater.

Virgil's first thought: it was on account of Frank Miller. The boy was ready this time and from now on would always be ready.

He phoned the undertaker who came with sheriff's people and pretty soon two deputy US marshals arrived, Virgil knowing them as serious lawmen in their dark suits and the way they cocked their soft felt hats down on their eyes. The marshals took over, the one who turned out to be the talker saying this Wally Tarwater – now lying in the hearse – was wanted on federal charges of running off livestock and crossing state lines to sell to meat packers. He said to Carlos to go on and tell in his own words what happened.

Virgil saw Carlos start to grin just a little, about to make some remark like, 'You want it in my own words?' and cut him off quick with, 'Don't tell no more'n you have to. These people want to get home to their families.'

Well, it began with Narcissa saying she felt like a rabbit stew, or squirrel if that's all was out there. 'I thought it was too late in the day,' Carlos said, 'but took a twenty-gauge and went out in the orchard. The pecans had been harvested, most of 'em, so you could see through the trees good.'

'Get to it,' Virgil said. 'You see this fella out in the pasture driving off your cows.'

'On a cutting horse,' Carlos said. 'You could tell this cowboy knew how to work beef. I got closer and watched him, admiring the way he bunched the animals without wearing himself out. I went back to the house and exchanged the twenty-gauge for a Winchester, then went to the barn and saddled up. She's right over there, the claybank? The sorrel's his.'

The marshal, the one who talked, said, 'You went back to get a rifle but don't know yet who he is?'

'I knew it wasn't a friend stealing my cows. He's driving them down towards the Deep Fork bottom, where a road comes in there. I nudge Suzie out among the cows still grazing, got close enough to call to him, "Can I help you?"' Carlos started to smile, 'He says, "Thanks for offering but I'm done here". I told him he sure was and to get down from his horse. He started to ride away and I fired one in the air to bring him around. I move closer but kept my distance, not knowing what he had under his slicker. By now he sees I'm young, he says, "I'm picking up cows I bought off your daddy". I tell him I'm the cattle outfit here, my dad grows pecans. All he says is, "Jesus, quit chasing me, boy, and go on home". Now he opens his slicker to let me see the six-shooter on his leg. And now, way off past him a good four hundred yards, I notice the stock trailer, a man standing there by the load ramp.'

'You can make him out,' the marshal who did the talking said, 'from that distance?'

'If he says it,' Virgil told the marshal, 'then he did.'

Carlos waited for the marshals to look at him before saying, 'The cowboy starts to ride off and I call to him to wait a second.

He reins and looks at me. I told him I'd quit chasing him if he brought my cows back. I said, "But you try to ride off with my stock I'll shoot you".'

'You spoke to him like that?' the talker said. 'How old are you?'

'Going on sixteen. The same age as my dad when he joined the marines.'

The quiet marshal spoke for the first time. He said, 'So this fella rode off on you?'

'Yes sir. Once I see he isn't gonna turn my cows, and he's approaching the stock trailer by now, I shot him.' Carlos dropped his tone saying, 'I meant to wing him, put one in the edge of that yellow slicker ... I should've stepped down 'stead of firing from the saddle. I sure didn't mean to hit him square. I see the other fella jump in the truck, doesn't care his partner's on the ground. He goes to drive off and tears the ramp from the trailer. It was empty, no cows aboard. What I did was fire the hood of the truck to stop it and the fella jumped out and ran for the trees.'

The talkative marshal spoke up. 'You're doing all this shooting from four hundred yards?' He glanced toward the Winchester leaning against a pecan tree. 'No scope on your rifle?'

'You seem to have trouble with the range,' Virgil said to him. 'Step out there about a hundred yards and hold up a live snake by its tail. My boy'll shoot its head off for you.'

'I believe it,' the quiet marshal said.

He brought a card from his vest pocket and handed it to Virgil between the tips of his fingers. He said, 'Mr Webster, I'd be interested to know what your boy sees himself doing in five or six years.'

Virgil looked at the card and then handed it to Carlos, meeting his eyes for a second. 'You want you can ask him,' Virgil said, watching Carlos reading the card that bore the deputy's name, R.C. 'Bob' Cardell, and a marshal's star in gold you could feel. 'I tell him join the marines and see foreign lands, or get to love pecans if you want to stay home.' He could see Carlos moving his thumb over the embossed star on the card. 'Tell you the truth, I don't think he knows yet what he wants to be when he grows up,' Virgil said to the marshal, and to Carlos, 'Isn't that right?'

Carlos raised his head.

'Sir, were you speaking to me?'

Later on, Virgil was in the living room reading the paper. He heard Carlos come down from upstairs and said, 'Will Rogers is appearing at the Hippodrome next week, with the Follies. You want to go see him?'

Carlos had his hand on his stomach. 'I don't feel so good. I upchucked my supper.'

Virgil lowered the newspaper to look at his boy. He said, 'You took a man's life today,' and watched Carlos nod his head thinking about it. 'You never said, but did you look at him laying there?'

'I got down to close his eyes.'

'Made you think, huh?'

'It did. I wondered why he didn't believe I'd shoot.'

'He saw you as a kid on a horse.'

'He knew stealing cows could get him shot or sent to prison. I mean anytime, but it's what he chose to do.'

'That's what you thought, looking at him? You didn't feel any sympathy for the man?'

'I did, I felt if he'd listened to me he wouldn't be lying there dead.'

The room was silent, and now Virgil asked, 'How come you didn't shoot the other one?'

'There weren't any cows on the trailer,' Carlos said, 'else I might've.'

It was his son's quiet tone that got to Virgil and made him realize, My Lord, but this boy has a hard bark on him.

II

June 13, 1927, Carlos Huntington Webster, now a six-footer, was in Oklahoma City wearing a new light-gray suit of clothes and a panama with the brim curved on his eyes just right, staying at a hotel, riding a streetcar for the first time, and being sworn in as a deputy United States marshal; while Lindbergh was being honored in New York City, tons of ticker tape dumped on the Lone Eagle for flying across the ocean; and Frank Miller, released from McAlester in bib overalls, was back in Checotah with Faye Harris, his suit hanging in the closet these six years since the marshals hauled him off in his drawers. The first thing Frank Miller did, once he got off of Faye, was make phone calls to get his gang back together.

Carlos was given leave to go home after his training and spent it with his old dad, telling him things:

What the room was like at the Huskin Hotel.

What he had to eat at the Plaza Grill.

How he saw a band called Walter Page's Blue Devils that was all colored guys.

How when firing a pistol you put your weight forward, one foot ahead of the other, so if you get hit you can keep firing as you fall.

And one other thing.

Everybody called him Carl instead of Carlos. At first he wouldn't answer to it and got in arguments, a couple of times almost fistfights.

'You remember Bob Cardell?'

'R.C. "Bob" Cardell,' Virgil said, 'the quiet one.'

'My boss now. He said. "I know you're named for your grand-daddy, to honor him, but you're using it like a chip on your shoulder instead of a name."'

Virgil was nodding his head. 'Ever since that moron Frank Miller called you a greaser. I know what Bob means. Like, "I'm Carlos Webster, what're you gonna do about it?" You were little I'd call you Carl sometimes. You liked it okay.'

'Bob Cardell says, "What's wrong with Carl? All it is, it's a nickname for Carlos".'

'There you are,' Virgil said. 'Try it on.'

'I've been wearing it the past month or so. "Hi, I'm Deputy US Marshal Carl Webster".'

'You feel any different?'

'I do, but I can't explain it.'

A call from Bob Cardell cut short Carl's leave. The Frank Miller Gang was back robbing banks.

What the marshals tried to do over the next few months was anticipate the gang's moves. They robbed banks in Shawnee, Seminole and Bowlegs on a line south. Maybe Ada would be next. No, it turned out to be Coalgate.

An eyewitness said he was in the barbershop as Frank Miller was getting a shave – except the witness didn't know who it was till later, after the bank was robbed. 'Him and the barber are talking, this one who's Frank Miller mentions he's planning on getting married pretty soon. The barber happens to be a minister of the Church of Christ and offers to perform the ceremony. Frank Miller says he might take him up on it and gives the reverend a five dollar bill for the shave. Then him and his boys robbed the bank.'

Coalgate was on that line south, but then they veered way over west to Kingfisher, took six thousand from the First National but lost a man: Jim Ray Monks, slow coming out of the bank on his bum legs, was shot down in the street. Before Monks knew he was dying he told them, 'Frank's sore you never put more'n five hundred on his head. He's out to show he's worth a whole lot more.'

The bank after Kingfisher was American National in Baxter Springs, way up on the Kansas line. The gang appeared to specialize in robbing banks in dinky towns – rush in with gunfire to get people's attention, and ride out with a hostage or two on the running board as a shield. Hit three or four banks in a row and then disappear for a time. There were reports of gang members spotted during these periods of lying low, but Frank Miller was never one of them.

'I bet anything,' Carl said, standing before the wall map in Bob Cardell's office, 'he hides out in Checotah, at Faye Harris's place.'

'Where we nabbed him,' Bob Cardell said, nodding, remembering. 'Faye was just a girl then, wasn't she?'

'I heard Frank was already seeing her,' Carl said, 'while she's married to Skeet, only Skeet didn't have the nerve to call him on it.'

'You heard, huh?'

'Sir, twice I drove down to McAlester on my day off, see what I could find out about Frank Miller.'

'The convicts talk to you?'

'One did, a Creek use to be in his gang. He said it wasn't a marshal shot Skeet Harris in the gun battle that time. It was Frank

Miller himself, to get Skeeter out of the way so he could have his wife.'

'You learned this on your own?'

'Yes sir. It was after that witness in Coalgate said he spoke of getting married. I thought it must be to Faye – don't you think? I mean if he's so sweet on her he killed her husband? That's what tells me he hides out there.'

Bob Cardell said, 'Well, we been talking to people, watching every place he's known to frequent. Look it up, I'm sure Faye Harris is on the list.'

'I did,' Carl said. 'She's checked off as having been questioned and deputies are keeping an eye on her place. But I doubt they do more than drive past, see if Frank Miller's drawers are hanging on the line.'

'You're a marshal four months,' Bob Cardell said, 'and you know everything.'

Carl didn't speak, Bob Cardell staring at him.

Bob Cardell saying after a few moments, 'I recall the time you shot that cattle thief off his horse at four hundred yards.' Bob Cardell saying after another silence but still holding Carl with his stare, 'You have some kind of scheme you want to try.'

'I've poked around and learned a few things about Faye Harris,' Carl said, 'where she used to live and all. I believe I can get her to talk to me.'

Bob Cardell said, 'How'd you get so sure of yourself?'

Marshals dropped Carl off a quarter mile from the house, turned the car around and drove back to Checotah; they'd be at the Shady Grove Café. Carl was wearing work clothes and boots, his .38 Special holstered beneath a limp old suitcoat of Virgil's, a black one, his star in a pocket.

Walking the quarter mile, his gaze held on this worn out homestead, the whole dismal hundred and sixty looking deserted, the dusty Ford coupe in the backyard abandoned. Carl expected Faye Harris to be in no better shape than her property, living here like an outcast. The house did take on life as he mounted the porch, the voice of Uncle Dave Macon coming from a radio somewhere inside; and now Faye Harris was facing him through the screen, a girl in a silky nightgown that barely came to her knees, barefoot, but with rouge, giving her face color and her blonde hair marcelled like a movie star's . . .

You dumbbell, of *course* she hadn't let herself go, she was waiting for a man to come and marry her. Carl smiled, meaning it.

'Miz Harris, I'm Carl Webster.' He kept looking at her face so she wouldn't think he was trying to see through her nightgown, which he could, easy. 'I believe your mom's name is Atha Trudell? She worked at the Georgian Hotel in Henryetta doing rooms at one time and belonged to Eastern Star?'

It nudged her enough to say, 'Yeah . . . ?'

'So'd my mom, Narcissa Webster?'

Faye shook her head.

'Your daddy was a coalminer up at Spelter, pit boss on the Little Gem. He lost his life that time she blew in '16. My dad was down in the hole laying track.' Carl paused. 'I was ten years old.'

Faye said, 'I just turned fifteen,' her hand on the screen door to open it, but then hesitated. 'Why you looking for me?'

'Lemme tell you what happened,' Carl said. 'I'm at the Shady Grove having a cup of coffee, the lady next to me at the counter says she works at a café serves way better coffee'n here. Purity's, up at Henryetta.'

Faye said, 'What's her name?'

'She never told me.'

'I use to work at Purity.'

'I know, but wait,' Carl said. 'The way you came up in the conversation, the lady says her husband's a miner up at Spelter. I tell her my dad was killed there in '16. She says a girl at Purity lost her daddy in that same accident. She mentions knowing the girl's mom from Eastern Star, I tell her mine belonged too. The waitress behind the counter's pretending not to listen, but now she turns to us and says, "The girl you're talking about lives right up the road there".'

'I bet I know which one it was,' Faye said. 'She have kind of a Betty Boop hair style?'

'I believe so.'

'What else she say?'

'You're a widow, lost your husband.'

'She tell you marshals gunned him down?'

'Nothing about that.'

'It's what everybody thinks. She mention any other names?'

What everybody thinks. Carl put that away and said, 'No, she got busy serving customers.'

'You live in Checotah?'

He told her Henryetta, he was visiting his old grandma, about to pass. She asked him, 'What's your name again?' He told her and she said, 'Well, come on in, Carl, and have a glass of ice tea.' Sounding now like she wouldn't mind company.

There wasn't much to the living room besides a rag rug on the floor and stiff black furniture, chairs and a sofa, their cane seats giving way from years of being sat on. The radio was playing in the kitchen. Faye went out there and pretty soon Carl could hear her chipping ice. He stepped over to a table laid out with magazines, *True Confession, Photoplay, Liberty, Dime Western,* one called *Spicy* . . .

Her voice reached him asking, 'You like Gid Tanner?'

Carl recognized the radio music. He said, 'Yeah, I do,' as he looked at pictures in *Spicy* of girls doing housework in their underwear, one girl up on a ladder in teddies with a feather duster.

'Gid Tanner and his Skillet Lickers,' Faye's voice said. 'You know who I kinda like? That Al Jolson, he sure sounds like a nigger on that mammy song. But you want to know who my very favorite is?'

Carl said, 'Jimmy Rogers?' looking at pictures of Joan Crawford and Elissa Landi now in *Photoplay*.

'I like Jimmy o-*kay* ... How many sugars?'

'Three'll do'er. How about Uncle Dave Macon? He was on just a minute ago.'

'"Take Me Back to My Old Carolina Home". I don't care for the way he half-sings and half-talks a song. If you're a singer you oughta sing. No, my favorite's Maybelle Carter and the Carter family. The pure loneliness she gets in her voice just tears me up.'

'Must be how you feel,' Carl said, 'living out here.'

She said, 'Don't give it another thought.'

'Sit here by yourself reading magazines ...'

'Honey,' Faye said, 'You're not as cute as you think you are. Drink your ice tea and beat it.'

'I'm sympathizing with you,' Carl said. 'The only reason I came, I wondered if you and I might even've known each other from funerals, and our moms being in the same club ... That's all.' He smiled just a little saying, 'I wanted to see what you look like.'

Faye said, 'All right, you *are* cute, but don't get nosy.'

She left him with his iced tea and went in the bedroom. Now what? Carl took *Photoplay* across the room to sit in a chair facing the table of magazines and the bedroom door, left open. He turned pages in the magazine. It wasn't a minute later she stuck her head out.

'You've been to Purity, haven't you?'

'Lot of times.'

She stepped into plain sight now wearing a pair of sheer, peach-colored teddies, the crotch sagging beneath her white thighs. Faye said, 'You hear about the time Pretty Boy Floyd came in?'

Carl could see London, he could see France ... 'While you were working there?'

'Since then, not too long ago. The word got around Pretty Boy Floyd was at Purity and it practically shut down the whole town. Nobody'd come out of their house.' She stood with hands on her hips in kind of a slouch. 'I did meet him one time. Was at a speak in Oklahoma City.'

'You talk to him?'

'Yeah, we talked about ... you know, different things.' She looked like she might be trying to think of what they did talk about, but said then, 'Who's the most famous person you ever met?'

He wasn't expecting the question. Still, he thought about it for no more than a few seconds before telling her, 'I guess it would have to be Frank Miller.'

Faye said, 'Oh ...?' like the name didn't mean much to her. Carl could tell, though, she was being careful, on her guard.

'Was in a drugstore when I was a kid,' Carl said, 'and Frank Miller came in for a pack of Luckies. I'd stopped there for a peach ice cream cone, my favorite. You know what Frank Miller did? Asked could he have a bite – this famous bank robber.'

'You give him one?'

'I did, and you know what? He kept it, wouldn't give me back my cone.'

'He ate it?'

'Licked it a few times and threw it away.' Carl didn't mention the trace of ice cream on Frank Miller's mustache; he kept that for himself. 'Yeah, he took my ice cream cone, robbed the store and shot a policeman. You believe it?'

She seemed to nod, thoughtful now, and Carl decided it was time to come out in the open.

'You said people think it was marshals gunned down your husband Skeet. But you know better, don't you?'

He had her full attention, staring at him now like she was hypnotized.

'And I'll bet it was Frank himself told you. Who else'd have the nerve? I'll bet he said you ever leave him he'll hunt you down and kill you. On account of he's so crazy about you. I can't think of another reason you'd stay here these years. You have anything to say to that?'

Faye began to show herself, saying, 'You're not from a newspaper ...'

'Is that what you thought?'

'They come around. Once they're in the house they can't wait to leave. No, you're not at all like them.'

Carl said, 'Faye, I'm a deputy United States marshal. I'm here to put Frank Miller under arrest or in the ground.'

III

He worried she might've acquired an affection for the man, but it wasn't so. Once Carl showed her his star, Faye sat down and breathed with relief. Pretty soon her nerves did take hold and she became talkative. Frank had phoned this morning and was coming. Now what was she supposed to do? Carl asked what time she expected him. She said going on dark. A car would drive past and honk twice; if the front door was open when it drove past again Frank would jump out and the car would keep going. Carl said he'd be sitting here reading about Joan Crawford. He said introduce him as a friend of the family happened to stop by, but try not to talk too much. He asked if Frank brought the magazines. She said they were supposed to be her treat. He asked out of curiosity if Frank could read. Faye said she wasn't sure, but believed he only looked at the pictures. What was it Virgil called him that time, years ago? A bozo.

He said to Faye, 'What you want to do is pay close attention. Then later on you can tell what happened here as the star witness and get your name in the paper. I bet even your picture.'

'I hadn't thought of that,' Faye said. 'You really think so?'

They heard the car beep twice as it passed the house.

Ready?

Carl was, in the chair facing the magazine table where the only lamp in the room was lit. Faye stood smoking a cigarette, smoking three or four since drinking the orange-juice glass of gin to settle her down. Light from the kitchen, behind her, showed her figure in the kimono she was wearing. Faye looked fine to Carl.

But not to Frank Miller. Not the way he came in with magazines under his arm and barely paused before saying to her, 'What's wrong?'

'Nothing,' Faye said. 'Frank, I want you to meet Carl, from home.' Frank staring at him now as Faye said he was a busboy at Purity the same time she was working there. 'And our moms are both Eastern Star.'

'You're Frank,' Carl said, sounding like a salesman. 'Glad to know you, Frank.' Carl looking at a face from six years ago, the same dead-eyed stare beneath the hat brim. He watched Frank Miller carry his magazines to the table, drop them on top of the ones there and glance over at Faye; watched him plant both hands on the table now, hunched over, taking time to what, rest? Unh-unh, decide how to get rid of this busboy so he could take Faye to bed, Carl imagining Frank doing it to her with his hat still on ... And remembered his dad saying, 'You know why I caught the Mauser round that time, the Spanish sniper picking me off? I was thinking instead of paying attention, doing my job.'

Carl asked himself what he was waiting for. He said, 'Frank, bring out your pistol and lay it there on the table.'

Faye Harris knew how to tell it. She had recited her story enough times to marshals and various law enforcement people. This after-noon she was describing the scene to newspaper reporters – and the one from the *Oklahoman*, the Oklahoma City paper, kept interrupting, asking questions that were a lot different than ones the marshals asked.

She referred to Deputy Marshal Webster as 'Carl' and the one from the *Oklahoman* said, 'Oh, you two are on intimate terms now? You don't mind he's just a kid? Has he visited you here at the hotel?' Faye was staying a few days at the Georgian in Henryetta. The other reporters in the room would tell the *Okla-homan* to keep quiet for Christ sake, anxious for Faye to get to the gunplay.

'As I told you,' Faye said, 'I was in the doorway to the kitchen. Frank's over here to my left, and Carl's opposite him but sitting down, his legs stretched out in his cowboy boots. I couldn't believe how calm he was.'

'What'd you have on, Faye?'

The *Oklahoman* interrupting again, some of the other reporters groaning.

'I had on a pink and red kimono Frank got me at Kerr's in Oklahoma City. I had to wear it whenever he came.'

'You have anything on under it?'

Faye said, 'None of your beeswax.'

The *Oklahoman* said his readers had a right to know such details of how a gun moll dressed. This time the other reporters were quiet, like they wouldn't mind hearing such details themselves, until Faye said, 'If this big mouth opens his trap one more time I'm through and y'all can leave.' She said, 'Now where was I?'

'Frank was leaning on the table.'

'That was it. He looked over at me like he was gonna say something, and right then Carl said, "Frank?" He said, "Draw your pistol and lay it there on the table".'

The reporters wrote it down in their notebooks and then waited as Faye took a sip of iced tea.

'I told you Frank had his back to Carl? Now I see him turn his face to his shoulder and say to him, "Do I know you from someplace?" Frank asks him, "Have we met or not?" And Carl says, "If I told you, I doubt you'd remember." Then – this is where Carl says, "Frank, I'm a deputy United States marshal. I'll tell you one more time to lay your pistol on the table".'

A reporter said, 'Faye, I know they did meet. I'm from the Okmulgee *Daily Times* and I wrote the story about it. Was six years ago to the month.'

'What you're doing,' Faye said, 'is holding up my getting to the good part.' Messing up her train of thought, too.

'But the circumstances of how they met,' the reporter said, 'could have something to do with this story.'

'Would you *please*,' Faye said, 'wait till I'm done?'

It gave her time to tell the next part: how Frank had no choice but to draw his gun, this big pearl-handle automatic, from inside his coat and lay it on the edge of the table, right next to him. 'Now as he turns around,' Faye said, starting to grin, 'this surprised look came over his face. He sees Carl sitting there, not with a gun in his hand but *Photoplay* magazine. Frank can't believe his eyes. He says, "Jesus Christ, you don't have a gun?" Carl pats the side of his chest where his gun's holstered under his coat and says, "Right here". Then he says, "Frank, I want to be clear about this so you understand. If I pull my weapon I'll shoot to kill".' Faye said to the reporters, 'In other words, the only time Carl Webster draws his gun it's to shoot somebody dead.'

It had the reporters scribbling in their note books and making remarks to each other, the one from the *Daily Times* saying now, 'Listen, will you? Six years ago Frank Miller held up Deering's drugstore in Okmulgee and Carl Webster was there. Only he was known as Carlos then, he was still a kid. He stood by and watched Frank Miller shoot and kill an Indian from the tribal police happened to come in the store, a man Carl Webster must've known.' The reporter looked at Faye and said, 'I'm sorry to interrupt, but I think the drugstore shooting could've been on Carl Webster's mind.'

Faye said, 'I can tell you something else about that.'

But now voices were chiming in, commenting and asking questions about the Okmulgee reporter's views:

'Carl carried it with him all these years?'

'Did he remind Frank Miller of it?'

'You're saying the tribal cop was a friend of his?'

'Both from Okmulgee, Carl thinking of becoming a lawman?'

'Carl ever say he was out to get Frank Miller?'

'This story's bigger'n it looks.'

Faye said, 'You want to hear something else happened? How Carl was eating an ice cream cone that time and what Frank did?'

They sat on the porch sipping tequila at the end of the day, insects out there singing in the dark. A lantern hung above Virgil's head so he could see to read the newspapers on his lap.

'Most of it seems to be what this little girl told.'

'They made up some of it.'

'Jesus, I hope so. You haven't been going out with her, have you?'

'I drove down, took her to Purity a couple times.'

'She's a pretty little thing. Has a saucy look about her in the pictures, wearing that kimona.'

'She smelled nice, too,' Carl said.

Virgil turned his head to him. 'I wouldn't tell Bob Cardell that. One of his marshals sniffing around a gun moll.' He waited, but Carl let that one go. Virgil looked at the newspaper he was holding. 'I don't recall you were ever a buddy of Junior Harjo's.'

'I'd see him and say hi, that's all.'

'The *Daily Times* has you two practically blood brothers. What you did was avenge his death. They wonder if it might even be the reason you joined the marshals.'

'Yeah, I read that,' Carl said.

Virgil put down the *Daily Times* and slipped the *Oklahoman* out from under it. 'But now the Oklahoma City paper says you shot Frank Miller 'cause he took your ice cream cone that time in the drugstore. They trying to be funny?'

'I guess,' Carl said.

'They could make up a name for you, as smart aleck newspapers do, start calling you Carl Webster, the Ice Cream Kid?'

'What if they do?'

'I'm getting the idea you like this attention.'

Virgil saying it with some concern and Carl giving him a shrug. Virgil picked up another paper from the pile. 'Here they quote the little girl saying Frank Miller went for his gun and you shot him through the heart.'

'I thought they have her saying, "straight through the heart",'

Carl said. He turned to see his old dad staring at him with a solemn expression. 'I'm kidding with you. What Frank did, he tried to bluff me. He looked toward Faye and called her name, thinking I'd look over. But I kept my eyes on him, knowing he'd pick up his Colt. He came around with it and I shot him.'

'As you told him you would,' Virgil said. 'Every one of the newspapers played it up, your saying, "If I draw my weapon I shoot to kill". You tell 'em that?'

'The only one I told was Frank Miller,' Carl said. 'It had to've been Faye told the papers.'

'Well, that little girl sure tooted your horn for you.'

'She only told what happened.'

'All she had to. It's the telling that did it, made you a famous lawman overnight. You think you can carry a load like that?'

'I was born to,' Carl said, starting to show himself.

It didn't surprise his old dad. Virgil picked up his glass of tequila and raised it to his boy, saying, 'God help us showoffs.'

Louly and Pretty Boy

Elmore Leonard

Here are some dates in Louly Ring's life from 1914, the year she was born in Tulsa, Oklahoma, to 1932, when she ran away from home to meet Joe Young, following his release from the Missouri State Penitentiary.

In 1918 her daddy, a Tulsa stockyard hand, joined the US Marines and was killed at Bois de Belleau during the World War. Her mom, sniffling as she held the letter, told Louly it was a woods over in France.

In 1920 her mom married a hardshell Baptist by the name of Otis Bender and they went to live on his cotton farm near Sallisaw, south of Tulsa on the other side of the Cookson Hills. By the time Louly was 12, her mom had two sons by Otis and Otis had Louly out in the fields picking cotton. He was the only person in the world who called her by her Christian name, Louise. She hated picking cotton but her mom wouldn't say anything to Otis. Otis believed that when you were old enough to do a day's work, you worked. It meant Louly finished with school by the sixth grade.

In 1924, that summer, they attended her cousin Ruby's wedding in Bixby. Ruby was 16, the boy she married, Charlie Floyd, 20. Ruby was dark but pretty, showing Cherokee blood from her mama's side. Because of their age difference Louly and Ruby had nothing to say to each other. Charlie called her kiddo and would lay his hand on her head and muss her bobbed hair that was sort of reddish, from her mom. He told her she had the biggest brown eyes he had ever seen on a little girl.

In 1925 she began reading about Charles Vincent Floyd in the paper: how he and two others went up to St Louis and robbed the Kroger Food payroll office of $11,500. They were caught in Ft Smith, Arkansas, driving around in a brand-new Studebaker. The Kroger Food paymaster identified Charlie saying, 'That's him, the pretty boy with apple cheeks.' The newspapers ate it up and referred to Charlie from then on as Pretty Boy Floyd.

Louly remembered him from the wedding as cute with wavy hair, but kind of scary the way he grinned at you – not being sure what he was thinking. She bet he hated being called Pretty Boy. Looking at his picture she cut out of the paper Louly felt herself getting a crush on him.

In 1929, while he was still in the penitentiary, Ruby divorced him on the grounds of neglect and married a man from Kansas. Louly thought it was terrible, Ruby betraying Charlie like that. 'Ruby don't see him ever again going straight,' her mom said. 'She needs a husband the same as I did to ease the burdens of life, have a father for her little boy, Dempsey.' Born in December of '24 and named for the world's heavyweight boxing champ.

Now that Charlie was divorced, Louly wanted to write and sympathize but didn't know which of his names to use. She had heard his friends called him Choc, after his fondness for Choctaw Beer, his favorite beverage when he was in his teens and roamed Oklahoma and Kansas with harvest crews. Her mom said it was where he first took up with bad companions, 'those drifters he met at harvest time,' and later on, working oil leases.

Louly opened her letter 'Dear Charlie,' and said she thought it was a shame Ruby divorcing him while he was still in prison, not having the nerve to wait till he was out. What she most wanted to know, 'Do you remember me from your wedding?' She stuck a picture of herself in a bathing suit, standing sideways and smiling over her shoulder at the camera. This way her 14–year-old breasts, coming along, were seen in profile.

Charlie wrote back saying sure he remembered her, 'the little girl with the big brown eyes'. Saying, 'I'm getting out in March and going to Kansas City to see what's doing. I have given your address to an inmate here by the name of Joe Young who we call Booger, being funny. He is from Okmulgee but has to do another year or so in this garbage can and would like to have a pen pal as pretty as you are.'

Nuts. But then Joe Young wrote her a letter with a picture of himself taken in the yard with his shirt off, a fairly good-looking bozo with big ears and blondish hair. He said he kept her bathing-suit picture on the wall next to his rack so he'd look at it before going to sleep and dream of her all night. He never signed his letters Booger, always, 'With love, your Joe Young'.

Once they were exchanging letters she told him how much she hated picking cotton, dragging that duck sack along the rows all day in the heat and dust, her hands raw from pulling the bolls off the stalks, gloves after a while not doing a bit of good. Joe said in his letter, 'What are you, a nigger slave? You don't like picking cotton, leave there and run away. It is what I done.'

In 1931 he said in a letter, 'I am getting my release sometime next summer. Why don't you plan on meeting me so we can get together.' Louly said she was dying to visit Kansas City and St Louis, wondering if she would ever see Charlie Floyd again. She asked Joe why he was in prison and he wrote back to say, 'Honey, I'm a bank robber, same as Choc.'

She had been reading more stories about Pretty Boy Floyd. He had returned to Akins, his hometown, for his daddy's funeral – *Akins only seven miles from Sallisaw* – his dad shot by a neighbor during an argument over a pile of lumber. When the neighbor disappeared there were people who said Pretty Boy had killed him. Seven miles away, and she didn't know it till after.

There was his picture again. PRETTY BOY FLOYD ARRESTED IN AKRON for bank robbery. Sentenced to 15 years in the Ohio State Penitentiary. Now she'd never see him but at least could start writing again.

A few weeks later another picture. PRETTY BOY FLOYD ESCAPES ON WAY TO PRISON. Broke a window in the toilet and jumped off the train and by the time they got it stopped he was gone.

It was exciting just trying to keep track of him, Louly getting chills and thrills knowing everybody in the world was reading about this famous outlaw she was related to – by marriage but not blood – this desperado who liked her brown eyes and had mussed her hair when she was a kid.

Now another picture. PRETTY BOY FLOYD IN SHOOTOUT WITH POLICE. Outside Uhlman's clothing store in Toledo, Ohio, and got away. There with a woman named Juanita – Louly not liking the sound of that.

Joe Young wrote to say, 'I bet Choc is through with Ohio and will never go back there.' But the main reason he wrote was to tell her, 'I am getting my release the end of August. I will let you know soon where to meet me.'

Louly had been working winters at Harkrider's grocery store in Sallisaw for six dollars a week, part time. She had to give five of it to Otis, the man never once thanking her, leaving a dollar to put in her running-away kitty. From the winter of 1930 to the fall of '32, working at the store most of six months a year, she hadn't saved a whole lot but she was going. She might have her timid-soul mom's looks, the reddish hair, but had the nerve and get-up-and-go of her daddy, killed in action charging a German machine gun nest in that woods in France.

Late in October, who walked in the grocery store but Joe Young. Louly knew him even wearing a suit, and he knew her, grinning as he came up to the counter, his shirt wide open at the neck. He said, 'Well, I'm out.'

She said, 'You been out two months, haven't you?'

He said, 'I been robbing banks. Me and Choc.'

She thought she had to go to the bathroom, the urge coming over her in her groin and then gone. Louly gave herself a few moments to compose herself and act like the mention of Choc didn't mean anything special, Joe Young staring in her face with his grin, giving her the feeling he was dumb as dirt. Some other convict must've wrote his letters for him. She said in a casual way, 'Oh, is Charlie here with you?'

'He's in Henryetta,' Joe Young said, looking toward the door. 'You ready? We gotta go.'

She said, 'I like that suit on you,' giving herself time to think. The points of his shirt collar spread open to his shoulders, his hair long on top but skinned on the sides, his ears sticking out, Joe Young grinning like it was his usual dopey expression. 'I'm not ready just yet,' Louly said. 'I don't have my running-away money with me.'

'How much you save?'

'Thirty-eight dollars.'

'Jesus, working here two years?'

'I told you, Otis takes most of my wages.'

'You want, I'll crack his head for him.'

'I wouldn't mind. The thing is, I'm not leaving without my money.'

Joe Young looked at the door as he put his hand in his pocket saying, 'Little girl, I'm paying your way. You won't need the thirty-eight dollars.'

Little girl – she stood a good two inches taller than he was, even in his run-down cowboy boots. She was shaking her head now. 'Otis bought a Model A Roadster with my money, paying it off twenty a month.'

'You want to steal his car?'

'It's mine, ain't it, if he's using my money?'

Louly had made up her mind and Joe Young was anxious to get out of here. She had pay coming, so they'd meet November first – no, the second – at the Georgian Hotel in Henryetta, in the coffee shop around noon.

The day before she was to leave, Louly told her mom she was sick. Instead of going to work she got her things ready and used the curling iron on her hair. The next day, while her mom was hanging wash, the two boys at school and Otis out in the field, Louly rolled the Ford Roadster out of the shed and drove into Sallisaw to get a pack of Lucky Strikes for the trip. She loved to smoke and had been doing it with boys but never had to buy the cigarettes. When boys wanted to take her in the woods she'd ask, 'You have Luckies? A whole pack?'

The druggist's son, one of her boyfriends, gave her a pack free of charge and asked where she was yesterday, acting sly, saying, 'You're always talking about Pretty Boy Floyd, I wonder if he stopped by your house.'

They liked to kid her about Pretty Boy. Louly, not paying close attention, said, 'I'll let you know when he does.' But then saw the boy about to spring something on her.

'The reason I ask, he was here in town yesterday, Pretty Boy Floyd was.'

She said, 'Oh?' careful now. The boy took his time and it was hard not to grab him by the front of his shirt.

'Yeah, he brought his family down from Akins, his mama, two of his sisters, some others, so they could watch him rob the bank. His grampa watched from the barber shop across the street. Bob Riggs, the bank assistant, said Pretty Boy had a tommy gun, but did not shoot anybody. He come out of the bank with $2,500.31, him and two other fellas. He gave some of the money to his people and they say to anybody he thought hadn't et in a while, everybody grinning at him. Pretty Boy had Bob Riggs ride on the running board to the end of town and let him go.'

This was the second time now he had been close by: first when his daddy was killed only seven miles away and now right here in Sallisaw, all kinds of people seeing him, damn it, but her. Just yesterday . . .

He knew she lived in Sallisaw. She wondered if he'd looked for her in the crowd watching.

She had to wonder, too, if she *had* been here would he of recognized her, and bet he would've.

She said to her boyfriend in the drug store, 'Charlie ever hears you called him Pretty Boy, he'll come in for a pack of Luckies, what he always smokes, and then kill you.'

The Georgian was the biggest hotel Louly had ever seen. Coming up on it in the Model A she was thinking these bank robbers knew how to live high on the hog. She pulled in front and a colored man in a green uniform coat with gold buttons and a peaked cap came around to open her door – and saw Joe Young on the sidewalk waving the doorman away, saying as he got in the car, 'Jesus Christ, you stole it, didn't you. Jesus, how old are you, going around stealing cars.'

Louly said, 'How old you have to be?'

He told her to keep straight ahead.

She said, 'You aren't staying at the hotel?'

'I'm at a tourist court.'

'Charlie there?'

'He's around someplace.'

'Well, he was in Sallisaw yesterday,' Louly sounding mad now, 'if that's what you call *around*,' seeing by Joe Young's expression she was telling him something he didn't know. 'I thought you were in his gang.'

'He's got an old boy name of Birdwell with him. I hook up with Choc when I feel like it.'

She was almost positive Joe Young was lying to her.

'Am I gonna see Charlie or not?'

'He'll be back, don't worry your head about it.' He said, 'We got this car, I won't have to steal one.' Joe Young in a good mood now. 'What we need Choc for?' Grinning at her close by the car. 'We got each other.'

It told her what to expect.

Once they got to the tourist court and were in No. 7, like a little one-room frame house that needed paint, Joe Young took off his coat and she saw the Colt automatic with a pearl grip stuck in his pants. He laid it on the dresser by a full quart of whiskey and two glasses and poured them each a drink, his bigger than hers. She stood watching till he told her to take off her coat and when she did, told her to take off her dress. Now she was in her white brassiere and panties. Joe Young looked her over before handing the smaller drink to her and clinking glasses.

'To our future.'

Louly said, 'Doing what?' Seeing the fun in his eyes.

He put his glass on the dresser, brought two .38 revolvers from the drawer and offered her one. She took it, big and heavy in her hand and said, 'Yeah . . .?'

'You know how to steal a car,' Joe Young said, 'and I admire that. But I bet you never held up a place with a gun.'

'That's what we're gonna do?'

'Start with a filling station and work you up to a bank.' He said, 'I bet you never been to bed with a grown man, either.'

Louly felt like telling him she was bigger than he was, taller, anyway, but didn't. This was a new experience, different than with boys her age in the woods, and she wanted to see what it was like.

Well, he grunted a lot and was rough, breathed hard through his nose and smelled of Lucky Tiger hair tonic, but it wasn't that much different than with boys. She got to liking it before he was finished and patted his back with her rough, cotton-picking fingers till he began to breathe easy again. Once he rolled off her she got her douche bag she'd taken out of Otis' grip and went in the bathroom, Joe Young's voice following her with, 'Whoooeee . . .'

Then saying, 'You know what you are now, little girl? You're what's called a gun moll.'

Joe Young slept a while, woke up still snockered and wanted to get something to eat. So they went to Purity, Joe said was the best place in Henryetta.

Louly said at the table, 'Charlie Floyd came in here one time. People found out he was in town and everybody stayed in their house.'

'How you know that?'

'I know everything about Charlie was ever written, some things only told.'

'Where'd he stay in Kansas City?'

'Mother Ash's boarding house on Holmes Street.'

'Who'd he go to Ohio with?'

'The Jim Bradley gang.'

Joe Young picked up his coffee he'd poured a shot into. He said, 'You're gonna start reading about me, chile.'

It reminded her she didn't know how old Joe Young was and took this opportunity to ask him.

'I'm thirty next month, born on Christmas Day, same as Baby Jesus.'

Louly smiled. She couldn't help it, seeing Joe Young lying in a manger with Baby Jesus, the three Wise Men looking at him funny. She asked Joe how many times he'd had his picture in the paper.

'When I got sent to Jeff City they's all kinds of pictures of me was in there.'

'I mean how many different times, for other stick-ups?'

She watched him sit back as the waitress came with their supper and he gave her a pat on the butt as she turned from the table. The waitress said, 'Fresh,' and acted surprised in a cute way. Louly was ready to tell how Charlie Floyd had his picture in the Sallisaw paper fifty-one times in the past year, once for each of the fifty-one banks robbed in that part of Oklahoma, all of them claiming Charlie as the bank robber. But if she told him, Joe Young would say Charlie couldn't of robbed that many since he was in Ohio part of '31. Which was true. An estimate said he might've robbed thirty-eight banks, but even that might cause Joe Young to be jealous and get cranky, so she let it drop and they ate their chicken-fried steaks.

Joe Young told her to pay the bill, a buck-sixty for everything including rhubarb pie for dessert, out of her running-away money. They got back to the tourist court and he screwed her again on her full stomach, breathing through his nose, and she saw how this being a gun moll wasn't all a bed of roses.

In the morning they set out east on Highway 40 for the Cookson Hills, Joe Young driving the Model A with his elbow out the window, Louly holding her coat close to her, the collar up against the wind, Joe Young talking a lot, saying he knew where Choc liked to hide. They'd go on up to Muskogee, cross the Arkansas and head down along the river to Braggs. 'I know the boy likes that country around Braggs.' Along the way he could hold up a filling station, show Louly how it was done.

Heading out of Henryetta she said, 'There's one.'

He said, 'Too many cars.'

Thirty miles later leaving Checotah, turning north toward Muskogee, Louly looked back and said, 'What's wrong with that Texaco station?'

'Something about it I don't like,' Joe Young said. 'You have to have a feel for this work.'

Louly said, 'You pick it.' She had the .38 he gave her in a black and pink bag her mom had crocheted for her.

They came up on Summit and crept through town, both of them looking, Louly waiting for him to choose a place to rob. She was getting excited. They came to the other side of town and Joe Young said, 'There's our place. We can fill up, get a cup of coffee.'

Louly said, 'Hold it up?'

'Look it over.'

'It's sure a dump.'

Two gas pumps in front of a rickety place, paint peeling, a sign that said EATS and told that soup was a dime and a hamburger five cents.

They went in while a bent-over old man filled their tank, Joe Young bringing his whiskey bottle with him, almost drained, and put it on the counter. The woman behind it was skin and bones, worn out, brushing strands of hair from her face. She placed cups in front of them and Joe Young poured what was left in the bottle into his.

Louly did not want to rob this woman.

The woman saying, 'I think she's dry.'

Joe Young was concentrating on dripping the last drops from his bottle. He said, 'Can you help me out?'

Now the woman was pouring their coffee. 'You want shine? Or I can give you Kentucky for three dollars.'

'Gimme a couple,' Joe Young said, drawing his Colt, laying it on the counter, 'and what's in the till.'

Louly did not want to rob this woman. She was thinking you didn't *have* to rob a person just cause the person had money, did you?

The woman said, 'Goddamn you, Mister.'

Joe Young picked up his gun and went around to open the cash register at the end of the counter. Taking out bills he said to the woman, 'Where you keep the whiskey money?'

She said, 'In there,' despair in her voice.

He said, 'Fourteen dollars?' holding it up, and turned to Louly. 'Put your gun on her so she don't move. The geezer come in, put it on him, too.' Joe Young went through a doorway to what looked like an office.

The woman said to Louly, pointing the gun from the crocheted bag at her now, 'How come you're with that trash? You seem like a girl from a nice family, have a pretty bag ... There something wrong with you? My Lord, you can't do better'n him?'

Louly said, 'You know who's a good friend of mine? Charlie

Floyd, if you know who I mean. He married my cousin Ruby.' The woman shook her head and Louly said, 'Pretty Boy Floyd,' and wanted to bite her tongue.

Now the woman seemed to smile, showing black lines between the teeth she had. 'He come in here one time. I fixed him breakfast and he paid me two dollars for it. You ever hear of that? I charge twenty-five cents for two eggs, four strips of bacon, toast and all you want of coffee, and he give me two dollars.'

'When was this?' Louly said.

The woman looked past Louly trying to see when it was and said, 'Twenty-nine, after his daddy was killed that time.'

They got the fourteen from the till and fifty-seven dollars in whiskey money from the back, Joe Young talking again heading for Muskogee, telling Louly it was his instinct told him to go in there. How was this place doing business, two big service stations only a few blocks away? So he'd brought the bottle in, see what it would get him. 'You hear what she said? "Goddamn you," but called me "Mister".'

'Charlie had breakfast in there one time,' Louly said, 'and paid her two dollars for it.'

'Showing off,' Joe Young said.

He decided they'd stay in Muskogee instead of going down to Braggs and rest up here.

Louly said, 'Yeah, we must've come a good fifty miles today.'

Joe Young told her not to get smart with him. 'I'm gonna put you in a tourist cabin and see some boys I know. Find out where Choc's at.'

She didn't believe him, but what was the sense of arguing?

It was early evening now, the sun going down.

The man who knocked on the door – she could see him through

45

the glass part – was tall and slim in a dark suit, a young guy dressed up, holding his hat at his leg. She believed he was the police, but had no reason, standing here looking at him, not to open the door.

He said, 'Miss,' and showed her his ID and a star in a circle in a wallet he held open, 'I'm Deputy US Marshal Carl Webster. Who am I speaking to?'

She said, 'I'm Louly Ring?'

He smiled straight teeth at her and said, 'You're a cousin of Pretty Boy Floyd's wife, Ruby, aren't you?'

Like getting ice-cold water thrown in her face, she was so surprised. 'How'd you know that?'

'We been making a book on Pretty Boy, noting down connections, everybody he knows. You recall the last time you saw him?'

'At their wedding, eight years ago.'

'No time since? How about the other day in Sallisaw?'

'I never saw him. But listen, him and Ruby are divorced.'

The marshal, Carl Webster, shook his head. 'He went up to Coffeyville and got her back. But aren't you missing an automobile, a Model A Ford?'

She had not heard a *word*, about Charlie and Ruby being back together. None of the papers ever mentioned her, just the woman named Juanita. Louly said, 'The car isn't missing, a friend of mine's using it.'

He said, 'The car's in your name?' and recited the Oklahoma license number.

'I paid for it out of my wages. It just happens to be in my stepfather's name, Otis Bender.'

'I guess there's some kind of misunderstanding,' Carl Webster said. 'Otis claims it was stolen off his property in Sequoyah County. Who's your friend borrowed it?'

She did hesitate before saying his name.

'When's Joe coming back?'

'Later on. 'Cep he'll stay with his friends he gets too drunk.'

Carl Webster said, 'I wouldn't mind talking to him,' and gave Louly a business card from his pocket with a star on it and letters she could feel. 'Ask Joe to give me a call later on, or sometime tomorrow if he don't come home. Y'all just driving around?'

'Seeing the sights.'

Every time she kept looking at him he'd start to smile. Carl Webster. She could feel his name under her thumb. She said, 'You're writing a book on Charlie Floyd?'

'Not a real one. We're collecting the names of anybody he ever knew that might want to put him up.'

'You gonna ask me if I would?'

There was the smile.

'I already know.'

She liked the way he shook her hand and thanked her, and the way he put on his hat, nothing to it, knowing how to cock it just right.

Joe Young returned about 9 a.m. making awful faces working his mouth, trying to get a taste out of it. He came in the room and took a good pull on the whiskey bottle, then another, sucked in his breath and let it out and seemed better. He said, 'I don't believe what we got into with those chickens last night.'

'Wait,' Louly said. She told him about the marshal stopping by, and Joe Young became jittery and couldn't stand still, saying, 'I ain't going back. I done ten years and swore to Jesus I ain't ever going back.' Now he was looking out the window.

Louly wanted to know what Joe and his buddies did to the

chickens, but knew they had to get out of here. She tried to tell him they had to leave, *right now.*

He was still drunk or starting over, saying now, 'They come after me, they's gonna be a shootout. I'm taking some of the scudders with me.' Maybe not even knowing he was playing Jimmy Cagney now.

Louly said, 'You only stole seventy-five dollars.'

'I done other things in the State of Oklahoma,' Joe Young said. 'They take me alive I'm facing fifteen years to life. I swear I ain't going back.'

What was going *on* here? They're driving around looking for Charlie Floyd – the next thing this dumbbell wants to shoot it out with the law and here she was in this room with him. 'They don't want *me*,' Louly said. Knowing she couldn't talk to him, the state he was in. She had to get out of here, open the door and run. She got her crocheted bag from the dresser, started for the door and was stopped by the bullhorn.

The electrified voice loud, saying, 'JOE YOUNG, COME OUT WITH YOUR HANDS IN THE AIR.'

What Joe Young did – he held his Colt straight out in front of him and started firing through the glass pane in the door. People outside returned fire, blew out the window, gouged the door with gunfire, Louly dropping to the floor with her bag, until she heard a voice on the bullhorn call out, 'HOLD YOUR FIRE.'

Louly looked up to see Joe Young standing by the bed with a gun in each hand now, the Colt and a .38. She said, 'Joe, you have to give yourself up. They're gonna kill both of us you keep shooting.'

He didn't even look at her. He yelled out, 'Come and get me!' and started shooting again, both guns at the same time.

Louly's hand went in the crocheted bag and came out with the

.38 he'd given her to help him rob places. From the floor, up on her elbows, she aimed the revolver at Joe Young, cocked it and *bam*, shot him through the chest.

Louly stepped away from the door and the marshal, Carl Webster, came in holding a revolver. She saw men standing out in the road, some with rifles. Carl Webster was looking at Joe Young curled up on the floor. He holstered his revolver, took the .38 from Louly and sniffed the end of the barrel and stared at her without saying anything before going to one knee to see if Joe Young had a pulse. He got up saying, 'The Oklahoma Bankers Association wants people like Joe dead, and that's what he is. They're gonna give you a five-hundred dollar reward for killing your friend.'

'He wasn't a friend.'

'He was yesterday. Make up your mind.'

'He stole the car and made me go with him.'

'Against your will,' Carl Webster said. 'Stay with that you won't go to jail.'

'It's true, Carl,' Louly said, showing him her big brown eyes. 'Really.'

The headline in the Muskogee paper, over a small photo of Louise Ring said SALLISAW GIRL SHOOTS ABDUCTOR.

According to Louise, she had to stop Joe Young or be killed in the exchange of gunfire. She also said her name was Louly, not Louise. The marshal on the scene said it was a courageous act, the girl shooting her abductor. 'We considered Joe Young a mad-dog felon with nothing to lose.' The marshal said that Joe Young was suspected of being a member of Pretty Boy Floyd's gang. He also mentioned that Louly Ring was related to Floyd's wife and acquainted with the desperado.

The headline in the Tulsa paper, over a larger photo of Louly, said GIRL SHOOTS MEMBER OF PRETTY BOY FLOYD GANG. The story told that Louly Ring was a friend of Pretty Boy's and had been abducted by the former gang member who, according to Louly, 'was jealous of Pretty Boy and kidnapped me to get back at him'.

By the time the story had appeared everywhere from Ft Smith, Arkansas, to Toledo, Ohio, the favorite headline was GIRL-FRIEND OF PRETTY BOY FLOYD GUNS DOWN MAD-DOG FELON.

The marshal, Carl Webster, came to Sallisaw on business and stopped in Harkrider's for a sack of Beechnut scrap. He was surprised to see Louly.

'You're still working here?'

'I'm shopping for my mom. No, Carl, I got my reward money and I'll be leaving here pretty soon. Otis hasn't said a word to me since I got home. He's afraid I might shoot him.'

'Where you going?'

'This writer for *True Detective* wants me to come to Tulsa. They'll put me up at the best hotel and pay fifty dollars for my story. Reporters from Kansas City and St Louis, Missouri, have already been to the house.'

'You're sure getting a lot of mileage out of knowing Pretty Boy, aren't you?'

'They start out asking about my shooting that dumbbell Joe Young, but what they want to know, if I'm Charlie Floyd's girlfriend. I say, "Where'd you get that idea?"'

'But you don't deny it.'

'I say, "Believe what you want, since I can't change your mind".'

What I wonder, you think Charlie's read about it and seen my picture?'

'Sure he has,' Carl said. 'I imagine he'd even like to see you again, in person.'

Louly said, 'Wow,' like she hadn't thought of that before this moment. 'You're kidding. Really?'

Comfort to the Enemy

Elmore Leonard

I

A German prisoner of war at the camp called Deep Fork had taken his own life, hanged himself two nights ago in the compound's washroom. Carl Webster was getting ready to look into it. Carl's boss, Bob McMahon, 17 years the United States marshal at Tulsa, said there was a question of whether the man did it on his own or was helped. McMahon shook his head over it.

'I doubt you'll learn what happened. He's a grenadier, the dead guy, Willi Martz. You ask about it, they look down their nose at you, deciding if they want to tell you anything.'

'I know what you mean,' Carl said. 'Some of 'em ever talk to you, it's like they're doing you a favor. But then they march off to work like the Seven Dwarfs singing the panzer song, "*Heiß über Afrikas Boden*". Or the one about Horst Wessel, that pimp they call a Nazi saint. I never saw a bunch of guys liked to sing so much. And they're serious about it. You imagine GIs singing like that?'

The POW camps in Oklahoma were full of Afrika Korps tank crewmen and grenadiers, most of them young and arrogant, hard-shell Nazis by the time they came out of Hitler Youth. A German soldier who wasn't a serious Nazi reported the Allied invasion of Normandy four months ago, read it to the Afrika Korps Nazis in the mess-hall from the front page of the *Okmulgee Daily Times*, and the Nazis called him a traitor and threw food at him and knocked him around for spreading enemy propaganda. The Africa veterans refused to believe they were losing the war; any reports of enemy victories had to be lies.

This could be what happened to Willi Martz: he was critical of the Führer, or called Goering a fat drug addict, and was lynched in the washroom.

Carl Webster stood before a map of America that covered an entire wall in Bob McMahon's office in the federal court building, Tulsa. Across nearly all of the forty-eight states were pushpins that showed the locations of the more than five hundred POW camps in the country; thirty-five in Texas, fifteen in Oklahoma, seventeen across the line in Arkansas, most of the camps in southern states, where enlisted men among the prisoners were put to work in farm labor, as allowed by the Geneva Convention.

Carl would be going to the camp near Okmulgee, his hometown, the one called Deep Fork after the river that ran through that part of the county and separated the camp from Carl's dad's property, a thousand acres of pecan trees and a dozen oil wells pumping for the war effort. Carl's dad Virgil Webster had been wealthy since the oil boom forty years ago, but didn't act like it. Texas Oil worked the half section they'd leased, paid Virgil in royalties while he tended his pecan trees and Carl, growing up, raised cows for beef, fed them a year and took them to market in a stock trailer. He was 15 when he shot a man trying to make off with his cows. There were stories in magazines about Carl and a book called *Carl Webster: the Hot Kid of the Marshals Service*, that told of his facing down fugitive offenders with the warning, 'If I have to pull my weapon I will shoot to kill'.

What Carl couldn't understand about the Afrika Korps guys – 250,000 of them walked over to the British lines in Tunisia and surrendered – they still believed they were winning the war. Carl would say to them, 'You quit fighting, didn't you? Climbed out of your tanks with your hands in the air?'

Yes, of course, but they seemed surprised by the question. They surrendered because they had no fuel for their tanks, no shells for the flak guns, the 88s they used on British armor. 'Once the RAF cut off our supply lines crossing the Mediterranean, what could we do?'

'When you give up,' Carl said, 'That's how you tell you're getting beat. And it's gonna get worse. There's no way in the world you guys are gonna win this war. You know how many Germans are here as prisoners? A good 350,000. You know how many Japanese we have in camps compared to you guys? Hardly any. You know why? Japs aren't allowed to surrender. It comes to that, they get out a hand grenade and pull the pin.'

Carl turned from the map of America to Bob McMahon at his desk, the lawman Carl first met when he shot the cow thief trying to make off with his stock. McMahon came by to investigate and heard how Carl had shot the trespasser out of his saddle at four hundred yards. McMahon gave Carl his card with the gold marshal's star on it Carl could feel under his thumb. Bob was 56 now, ready to retire and plant a victory garden, sit and watch his tomatoes grow.

Carl was married to Louly Brown, seven years now but no children; they were ready to start a family, the war came along to hold up their plans. At the time they met people believed Louly was Pretty Boy Floyd's girlfriend, not just a cousin of his wife's, and Louly let them believe it till she got tired of the act she was putting on.

In 1942 Carl was 36 when he tried to enlist in the First Cavalry

Division at Fort Hood, Texas, and was turned down because of his age and his irregular heartbeat. He tried using his influence as a famous lawman – news stories and the book written about him – a US marshal who had shot and killed a dozen armed offenders in the line of duty. He was told the First Cavalry did not have a regiment for inexperienced middle-aged men. Next he tried the Marine Corps, Virgil's choice when he ran away from home at 16, serving with the marine detachment aboard the battleship *Maine* when the dons blew her up in Havana harbor in February of '98; and was with Huntington's marines at Guantànamo when a Spanish sniper sent him home aboard the hospital ship *Solace*. Virgil wrote a letter to the Marines but it didn't do Carl any good. He was turned down. But now the sailor in the Tulsa recruiting office had an idea. 'You have a trade, you can join a navy construction battalion, the Seabees. They don't care how old you are.'

Carl went for it: joined the Navy, made it through boot camp and came out of advanced Seabee training at Port Hueneme, California, a Bosun's Mate First Class, assigned to Construction Battalion Maintenance Unit 585. In a letter home he told Louly most of these guys had no idea how to wear a sailor hat; he told her he'd gotten a tattoo, *Carlos*, on his left shoulder in blue script with red highlights, for a buck.

When they closed the apartment in Tulsa, Louly had moved in with Virgil, and his common-law wife Narcissa Raincrow, near Okmulgee. But now Louly wrote to say she felt she had to get out of their house, she didn't fit in with their ways. Louly said in her letter, 'You know how old your dad is? He's seventy. He sits all day with newspapers and gives you his opinion of world events, and I'm tired of nodding my head.'

To escape, Louly joined the Women Marines, which Virgil called the BAMs, the Big Ass Marines. By the time Carl was in New Guinea, ready to make the 200–mile jump to Los Negros in the Admiralty Islands, where CBMU 585 would maintain an air strip, Louly was a gunnery instructor at the Marine Air Base, Chapel Hill, NC.

Carl wrote to Louly from New Guinea saying, 'Believe it or not, the First Cavalry is the outfit that took Los Negros from the Japs, the first action in their history they didn't ride in on horses. The island is secure, the cavalry's waiting on us to come and get the airstrip in shape. General MacArthur referred to taking Los Negros as "putting the cork in the bottle," but I don't know what he meant by it.'

Barely two months later, on Los Negros, Carl became CBMU 585's first and only medals winner when he was shot by Japanese soldiers who weren't supposed to be there: a Purple Heart for his gunshot wounds and a Navy Cross for killing the last two Japs on the island. Carl said it was the only shootout he was in he didn't see coming. His wounds left him with a limp until his honorary discharge, back to wearing his marshal's star, by the end of June, 1944.

He told Louly in a letter he was amazed at the number of camps they'd built and all the POWs they brought over in the two years he was away.

'The troop ships take our boys to Europe and come back loaded with Germans. They're full-up in England, no room for any more – in case you were wondering who's winning the war. Are you still showing jarheads how to get the most out of a Browning machine gun?'

Carl said to his boss he'd talk to Jurgen before investigating the suicide – Jurgen Schrenk, a young captain who'd been a member of Rommel's reconnaissance team. He was one of the interpreters for the 2200 prisoners at Deep Fork, a camp for officers, noncoms and enlisted men, nearly all of them Afrika Korps.

'You'll have to find him first,' McMahon said. 'Jurgen's busted out again, the fourth time this year.'

'Four times that we know of,' Carl said. 'I think he slips out whenever he feels like it and gets back before he turns up missing. He has to be seeing some girl.'

'If he is,' McMahon said, 'and she knows he's a POW, she can be brought up on a charge of treason.'

'It's why he won't tell where he goes,' Carl said. 'I've talked to him enough. He sounds like some guy lives up the road, talks with hardly a speck of accent, but you can hear it if you listen. Like the way he says Ah-frica. You know he lived in Detroit a couple of years, in the thirties when his dad brought the family over. The dad was an engineer with Ford Motor in Germany, some kind of production expert. Jurgen was in his teens when they went home. Three years later he's driving a tank into Poland. 'Forty-one he went to North Africa with Rommel and he's been here since 'forty-three. He acts stuck-up if other POWs are around, but not to the point you want to hit him. He thinks he's smarter than I am.'

McMahon said, 'Is he?'

'He remembers what he reads and plays it back like it's something he thought of. I talk to Wesley about him. Wesley says if he's up to something besides seeing a girl, he doesn't know what it could be.'

Wesley was the former Adair County Sheriff, now Colonel Wesley Sellers, commander of the Deep Fork POW camp.

'That's right,' McMahon said, 'you and Wesley go back a ways.'

'He was with the posse the time we cornered Peyton Bragg and Peyton tried to run off on us. Wesley told the newspapers I shot Peyton with a Winchester driving away at four hundred yards, in the dark.'

'I remember,' McMahon said, 'and it was only what, three hundred? You always managed to have reliable witnesses.'

'People can't help but exaggerate wanting to tell a good story. What the Krauts do,' Carl said, 'is lie with a straight face thinking they're funny. You notice other Krauts standing around trying not to grin. Jurgen does it, but doesn't seem to care if you catch on. The thing about Jurgen, he's a likeable guy. He says he got along great with Rommel. Why wouldn't he? He gets along with everybody. Wesley says he could have Jurgen transferred to another camp, but what's the harm of his slipping out for a few days? He always comes back, doesn't he? There're camps where they even let the POW officers go out, as long as they stay within fifty miles.'

McMahon said, 'I'm not going to worry about it till I have to.'

Carl said, 'Not when you have a bigger percentage of inmates trying to bust out of federal prisons than these guys wandering off. They've never had it so good.'

Carl Webster had been dealing with POWs pretty much as a full-time job since coming home with his medals. The Provost Marshal's office in Washington had asked Carl to keep an eye on the POWs in Oklahoma. He talked to young officers like Jurgen and read what he could find on Adolf Hitler and the Wehrmacht, learning about the SS and the Gestapo, and got to see Nazi Party films on Hitler taking over Germany in 1934. Carl said they were fairly boring movies, hundreds of thousands of Krauts goose-stepping past Hitler and giving him the old Sieg Heil.

'Out of 360,000 German POWs in this country,' Carl said to McMahon, 'we get about a hundred escape attempts a month. That's three a day from the more than five hundred camps across the country. Jurgen says the easiest way is to walk off a work crew out on some farm. You know officers and noncoms don't have to work if they don't feel like it, but it's a way to get out of the camp. I met Jurgen for the first time, he was working for my dad, swatting pecans off the trees with a bamboo pole. Jurgen gets twenty a month for being an officer. Generals get forty bucks. I doubt any of them work. Von Arnim, who ran the show in North Africa? He's at Camp Clinton in Mississippi. It's one of the biggest camps we have, with ten generals there, each one with his own house and his orderlies. But the enlisted men, they're all out on farms working morning to night. Muskogee County, POWs work a month to bring in the spinach at harvest time.'

'They were farmers back home,' McMahon said. 'They miss it.'

'Jurgen showed me pictures he has from Tunisia. He's in his Afrika Korps shorts, the kind he wears all the time, no shirt on. He's grinning, wants you to see his perfect teeth. In one he's brushing his hair out of his eyes, bleached from the African sun, smiling, always smiling. I told him he could be a poster boy for the Happy Nazi Party. He says he was a Hitler Youth poster in 1936.'

'Tell him,' McMahon said, 'if he has a girlfriend it's okay, we won't bother her.'

'You mean till the war's over.'

'Some lonely farm girl,' McMahon said, 'doesn't care he's the enemy. Or he gets by playing he's American.'

'I think he could.'

'She picks him up on the highway and takes him home. She's alone, her husband could be off fighting Germans.'

Carl said, 'Two or three days with her, the MPs find him sitting in the OK Café, at the counter with 'PW' stenciled on the back of his shorts. He gets solitary and bread and water for a week. Jurgen told me escaping was a joke – nothing to it. He's still tan – I think he works at it. It gets cold, he puts on an overcoat with the shorts. In some of the Africa pictures that's what he's wearing, the overcoat over bare legs. Smiling. He's twenty-six, he's been a soldier going on six years.'

McMahon said, 'Well, you know him better than anyone else. How do you see him?'

Carl said, 'You hear of prisoners around Sallisaw picking cotton, doing that stoop work all day for eighty cents? That's what the government pays them. You can't tell me there aren't girls out in the cottonfield.'

'You think that's the case with Jurgen?'

'Seeing some girl could be all he's after,' Carl said. 'Still, I imagine him looking at ideas, dreaming up ways to use his energy. I see him as the kind of guy can't sit still. What I'll have to do is find out where he goes and see what that tells us.'

They talked about Willi Martz, the suicide, 28, unmarried. 'He might be a homosexual.' McMahon said. 'We know the Nazis like to pick on those fellas.'

'What we have to do,' Carl said, 'is separate the hard-nosed Nazis from the ones who don't take it seriously but go along. We weed out the bullies and send them to Alva, that camp in the western part of the state reserved for hard-core Nazis. See, the way we find out if a Kraut's a bona fide Nazi, we tell him a joke. The one, Adolf Hitler wants to know when he's gonna die, so he asks his astrologer. The astrologer tells him he's gonna die on a Jewish holiday. Hitler gets excited. He says, "Tell me, which one"? The astrologer says, "Mein Führer, any day you die becomes a Jewish holiday". And if the guy we tell it to doesn't laugh, we send him to Alva.'

A young deputy by the name of Gary Marion, wearing an old-timer, narrow-brim Stetson, stepped into the doorway to McMahon's office.

'They're picking up the Kraut, the one escaped name of Jurgen?' Gary saying the name with a J sound, like Jergens Lotion. 'He's waiting in that café in his PW shorts.'

II

Norma, the waitress who'd spoken to Jurgen this time, waited for Carl Webster to drive down from Tulsa. They sat in a booth to talk about Jurgen always coming to the OK Café in Okmulgee, four times now, to give himself up.

Carl said, 'Why you suppose he comes here?'

'He likes the coffee? I don't know,' Norma said, smoking a cigarette. 'I waited on him 'cause I didn't get to talk to him the other time and I had something I wanted to say. The manager called the camp right away and that's all there was to it, the MPs came and picked him up. I been thinking, he must come here 'cause he knows he'll be safe. Nobody's going to come in and shoot him.'

'What'd you talk about?'

'As soon as he sat down I went to the counter to wait on him, I was anxious to tell him something. Here he is, Carl, the enemy, but doesn't look anymore like a foreigner than you do. His hair seems different, but that's about all. I planned to tell him, if we got to talk, my husband was with Patton's Fourth

Armored racing through France, but I didn't. I was polite and asked him how he liked Oklahoma. He said fine, but had expected to see mountains, Oklahoma being out west. The MPs came in pointing guns at him, but all they did was kid around, like they're sure he's seeing a girl. But you know what he told me? I have pretty eyes.'

'Yeah . . . ?' Carl smiling now.

He and Norma had graduated from Okmulgee High the same year, Carl a Bulldog in three sports while Norma hung around with guys behind the stands smoking cigarettes.

'Before the MPs came in he said, "Come here, closer," motioning to me. I leaned my arms on the counter right in front of him, and he reached over and pretended to pull a coin out of my ear, a dime, and gave it to me, with a nice smile you could see in his eyes.'

'Wanting you to trust him.'

'He said, "Thank you, Norma, for the coffee". He said my name.'

'It's on your uniform.'

'I know, but he took the trouble to say it, "Thank you, Norma," making it sound natural, like we'd known each other a while, or maybe were even pretty close at one time.'

Carl said, 'You got all that out of "Thank you, Norma?" He was giving you his ten cent magic trick.'

'With the smile,' Norma said.

'I've seen the smile. He's sure of himself, isn't he? But without sounding cocky. He doesn't put on any airs. He tell you anything about himself?'

'He wanted to know about *me*, if I lived alone. He didn't ask if I was married, only do I live alone.'

'Wants to know if you're available.'

'I told him my husband was with General Patton's armor

right this minute heading for Germany. You know what he said? "Patton, yes, with the discipline". He said when Patton came to Africa to command the Second Corps he made all his tank crewmen and infantrymen wear neckties. He said, "You know of course George Patton is German?" I said, "That's funny, I read he's Scottish and his people go back to the time of George Washington". You know what Jurgen said? "Yes, one or the other".'

'You catch him making something up,' Carl said, 'it doesn't bother him. Like it isn't important anyway.'

'I didn't know they had to wear ties,' Norma said. 'Bobby wasn't with Patton till after Normandy and never mentioned wearing a tie. If he did, he wouldn't of told me anyway, knowing what I think of George Patton.'

'How do you see him?'

'Carl, the man's a showoff, he wears a pair of six-shooters with ivory handles. But he can get guys like Bobby willing to die for him.' She kept tapping her cigarette in the ashtray. 'How come you weren't interested in Jurgen before?'

'We're starting to wonder if he's up to something.'

'Like what?'

'Some kind of sabotage. Set fire to storage tanks.'

Born on an oil lease, she knew what he was talking about. Norma said, 'On his own? He'd need help. I told you the guards think he has a girlfriend and the only reason he escapes, it's to get his ashes hauled. They're sure of it.'

'How come?'

''Cause whatever he's up to must be the kind of thing nobody ever sees you doing anyway. If you know what I mean.'

Carl said, 'You know the girl would have to live around here.'

''Course she would.'

Carl said, 'You might even know her.'
Norma said, 'Or you might if I don't.'

During the first World War, young Wesley Sellers showed he was alert and liked being in the US Army and made it up to captain without leaving Camp Polk, Louisiana. For this war he was brought back as a colonel in the Provost Marshal's office and appointed commander of the Deep Fork camp. He had told Carl sitting in his office he had five hundred German officers in one compound of thirty barracks, and 1700 non-commissioned officers and enlisted men in the other three compounds. All Carl could see, looking out the window and through the wire fences, were rows of tar-paper barracks down the left side of the road and gun towers around the perimeter. Wesley said he wanted the noncoms, not just the enlisted men out working during the day, even though it was up to them if they worked or not. So he made a deal with the staff officers: send all your boys out to work and the officers could have a soccer league and put on plays and musicals, have three-two beer served in the canteen and officer's club and their own chefs in the mess halls.

'Oh, they can look down their nose at you,' Wesley said, 'and make demands, chew you out they think you aren't living up to the Geneva Convention. I run this place like they're guests of my hotel, the Fritz Ritz, as long as they don't break any of the house rules, like hanging around near the fences. I tell my boys in the gun towers, you see a prisoner approaching the fence, yell at him twice to halt. He doesn't back off, shoot him. I tell the officers this is the way it's gonna be, and they understand, nod their Kraut heads, 'cause these people operate on unconditional discipline. They give an order, it's obeyed. I said to an officer I can speak freely to, "The war's over for you people, why do you keep playing

soldier? Why do you let a few hardcore Nazis push you around?"
This Kraut I can trust says, "Because they could be taking names,
making a list of the ones aren't arrogant enough".'

'Your guards shot any of 'em?'

'One. Held on to the fence and dared the tower guard to shoot
him, so he did. Other camps they've had to shoot prisoners. Up
in Kansas a Kraut ran out of bounds after a soccer ball and was
shot. He was told to halt, but kept going. Colorado, a guard back
from combat, shot three Krauts he said were coming for him.'

Wesley Sellers said he didn't worry about prisoners escaping.
He had reports that listed eleven hundred sneaking out of camps
or from work details during the past two years and nine hundred
of them were picked up in a couple of days. 'Some of them, soon
as they're hungry, they head back to camp.'

Carl said, 'What about Willi Martz?'

'I asked several of the highest ranking officers here why they
thought the man killed himself. They all said they didn't know,
or "How would I know?" Showing me they didn't care. I asked
some lieutenants and they said he was ashamed of himself, a moral
pervert who could not stand living with men who refused to speak
to him. I asked if Martz was anti-Nazi. They said of course he
was. I asked if he'd had any help hanging himself, since there
wasn't anything he could've been standing on he kicked out from
under him. I said it looked like some of you held him up while
you put the rope around his neck and then let go of him. One of
them said that would be a way to do it. They all said yah, nodding
their heads, grinning.'

'Be hard,' Carl said, 'to keep your composure.'

'When I was sheriff,' Wesley said, 'questioning an offender, say
a stickup guy, and he grinned at me like that? I'd punch him in
the mouth. Why I always had leather gloves on me I was investigating a crime. But I can't punch any of these Kraut officers, can

I? All dressed up in their uniforms with their medals and gee-gaws, their Iron Crosses.'

'I don't know if you can or not,' Carl said. 'I know the SS always beat up people they have in to question. Or pull out their fingernails.'

'I don't believe in torture,' Wesley said. 'All a punch in the mouth's for is to get their attention.'

'You talk to Jurgen since he's back?'

'I got him in what passes for solitary here, a room with a cot and a bucket, a narrow window that doesn't give much light. I could leave Jurgen in there till he tells me where he's been. Or, I could beat him up, I suppose, if I cared enough, but I don't.'

'I have to talk to him about the suicide.'

'Come back tomorrow,' Wesley said. 'Meantime, since you're close to home, go visit your old dad and sit on the porch with him.'

It's what Carl did, drove around to the big California bungalow in the pecan orchard, his dad 70 years old now but had not changed much in Carl's memory. They sat in wicker chairs on the porch, Carl and his dad Virgil with bottles of Mexican beer, a pile of newspapers on Virgil's lap. The beer and the newspapers were from the oil company that leased a half section of Virgil's property, Virgil's share of the royalties an eighth of whatever the oil company made.

They'd finish their beers and Virgil would raise his voice to say, 'Honey, what're you doing?' and Narcissa, 54 now, would come out to the porch with two more of whatever they were drinking. Narcissa Raincrow had been living here since she was 16, hired to wet-nurse Carl when his mother Graciaplena passed away two days after giving birth to him. That was in 1906. Virgil had married Grace and brought her here from Cuba after the war with Spain. Narcissa wasn't married but had delivered a child stillborn and needed to give her milk to a newborn infant, so it worked out.

When Carl first brought his wife Louly to the house he told her that by the time he had lost interest in Narcissa's breasts, his dad had acquired an appreciation, first keeping her on as housekeeper, then as his common-law wife for the past thirty-eight years. Virgil thought she looked like Dolores Del Rio, only was older, and heavier.

Virgil was telling Carl he wanted to hire a POW as a handyman for clean-up work, painting, whatever was needed done around the place. 'But the guy at the camp in charge of labor says I have to take three guys. He says the way it works, it's one guard for every three prisoners. He can't send a guard to watch one man. I said you don't have to send a guard, I'll watch the Hun myself. I'll give him a bottle of beer with lunch, he won't think of running off. The labor nitwit said it's one to three and wouldn't budge from it.'

Carl said, 'You remember Jurgen Schrenk? He worked here when you were gathering and shipping to wholesalers, the one I mentioned escaped every couple of months for a few days?'

'Yeah, and I spoke to him. I asked Jurgen if he went out to find something of a military nature he could sabotage. I told him I was aboard the USS *Maine* when the dons blew her up in Havana harbor, February 1898. I said I doubt he could cause an explosion as earthshaking as the *Maine* going down with 254 hands. It got us hurrying to go to war with Spain. Jurgen said he just liked to get away from the camp, walk down a road with no place to go. Oh, is that so? What do you bet he's got some farm girl thinks he stepped out of a dream in his short pants? The Huns look pretty much like us, except there's something different about them. People'd come by to watch them work. One time – they're swatting pecans along the county road – I noticed a car stopped nearby. Pretty soon a guard come along and told the woman in the car to keep moving. The reason I know it was a woman, Narcissa's coming from town in our car and slowed up going past the car stopped there. She said it was a girl with blonde hair but didn't recognize her from anyplace.'

Carl said, 'What about the car?'

'I thought it was a green Hudson with whitewalls. Nacissa says I don't know cars, it was a '39 Lincoln-Zephyr. She reads the car ads and tells me what we should get after the war. But listen, the guard that told the girl to keep moving? I saw him a few times while he was around here. His name's Larry Davidson. From West Memphis, Arkansas, the poor soul. Young guy, sees himself as a hotshot the way he wears his overseas cap. Talk to Larry. See what he says.'

'Yeah, it was a green Lincoln,' Larry said. 'I went over and told her she couldn't stop there.'

Larry Davidson was telling this to Carl outside the camp administration building where you could smoke, a big tin can for butts fixed to the rail along there. 'I told her she had to keep moving as these were enemy soldiers, German prisoners of war working here.' She said, "Oh my, are they really Germans?" Sounding like she was surprised.'

'Was she?'

'I thought she was putting it on.'

'She ask about any of the prisoners?'

'What she asked me,' Larry said, 'if they tried to run would

I shoot them? I told her it's why I had the carbine. She said, but they were just like us, they come from nice homes, they miss their wives and sweethearts—'

'She ask if you're friends with any of them?'

'She did. I said, "Are you nuts? Why would I want a Nazi for a friend?"'

Carl liked this boy from West Memphis, Arkansas. He asked him, 'How old would you say she is?'

'She's twenty-six,' Larry said, 'according to her drivers license. Here's a good-looking girl my age drives a Lincoln-Zephyr. I'm thinking, Hmmm, what have we here? I asked to see her license to get her name and address, but then talking to her she didn't seem like a whole lot of fun. She takes care of her mom, says she keeps her from becoming depressed. They live on Seminole Avenue in this great big house. Must've cost her, so I'd say she has money.'

'You went to see her?'

'Drove past the house is all. Her name's Shemane . . . I think Morrison.'

'Shemane Morrissey,' Carl said.

Larry said, 'You know her?'

'She was in all the papers ten years ago. A friend of mine wrote a feature story about her in *True Detective*,' Carl said. '"Tulsa Society Girl Abducted by White Slavers".'

Larry said, 'You're kidding me.'

'They took her to Kansas City and put her to work in a whorehouse.'

Larry said, 'Shemane?'

'Sixteen years old, all she was. But after a while, when she could've walked out? She didn't want to come home.'

'She got to like being a whore?'

'She liked Kansas City, the action, and got to like a guy who was high up in the machine that ran the city – the girl you didn't think would be much fun.'

Larry squinted at Carl. 'What's she done you're after her for?'

'She drive a green Lincoln?'

Larry nodded. 'With whitewalls.'

'The third time Jurgen escaped,' Carl said, 'a witness swears she saw Jurgen get out of a green car and duck into the OK Café.'

'You think Shemane's the one he's been seeing?'

'I'm gonna find out,' Carl said.

III

Carl spent the night at his dad's. The next morning, while they were having their bacon and eggs, Wesley Sellers called from the camp to say there was a deputy marshal by the name of Gary Marion in his office. 'Standing against my desk,' Wesley said. 'He wants to question Jurgen Schrenk and says he has the authority. You know this boy?'

Carl could hear Wesley's irritation. He asked him to put Gary on the phone. He waited and now Gary came on to say, 'Yes sir . . .?'

What Carl knew about Gary Marion, from some little town near Waco, Texas, he'd been a marshal less than two years, was 25 but tried to appear seasoned in his cowboy boots and Stetson, an old hat with a narrow brim he never took off. He wore this look on the short, stocky frame of a former rodeo bullrider, Gary's career before he joined the marshals. He said to Carl when they first met in the Tulsa office, 'You know what attracted me to law enforcement? I read your book, the one about you being the hot kid of the marshals service.' Carl said it wasn't his book, as he didn't write it. Gary said no matter, it had inspired him, given him the chills and thrills reading how Carl had faced fugitive outlaws and shot them down where they stood. He said to Carl, 'Are you still the hot kid? Or is it time somebody took your place?' Gary grinning but serious about what he was saying.

Talking to him on the phone in the kitchen, his dad and Narcissa watching, Carl said, 'What are you doing there?'

'I believe I can talk man to man with this Kraut,' Gary said, 'get him to spill where he's been. Me and him are the same age, Carl. He'll understand where I'm coming from and tell me what I want to know.'

Carl said, 'Put Colonel Sellers on.'

'Don't I have the authority as a federal agent,' Gary said, 'to talk to the Kraut if I suspect he's up to something?'

'No, you don't,' Carl said. 'Put Sellers on.'

It took a minute or so for Wesley to pick up the phone. 'I sent him outside to wait. Is this boy any good?'

'Put him in with Jurgen,' Carl said, 'and we'll find out.'

His dad watched him hang up the wall phone and return to the table in the back part of the kitchen, a view of pecan trees outside the windows. 'You been on the telephone since you got here,' Virgil said, 'talking long distance to that *True Detective* writer when I went to bed.'

'The one wrote the book,' Narcissa said, warming his coffee as Carl sat down. 'He hasn't been here in a while.'

Carl said, 'You remember a piece Tony Antonelli wrote some time ago, "Society Girl Abducted by White Slavers"?'

'Shemane Morrissey,' Virgil said. 'Nothing to it; the guard on the work detail gives you the name of the girl and you recall she was snatched from her home and taken to Kansas City,' Virgil nodding, remembering. 'It had something to do with her dad.'

'A Tulsa lawyer,' Carl said, 'who got rich representing oil money. They're in society, lived in Maple Ridge—'

'Alvin Morrissey,' Virgil said, using his memory of newspaper headlines, 'got involved with a honky-tonk girl from Kansas City. Gave her a pile of money to move to Tulsa and become his mistress. They're in a suite at the Mayo, in bed having a smoke after doing it, a guy comes in and shoots them. I remember reading the bed caught fire from their cigarettes. The maid threw a pitcher of ice water on it.'

'Alvin met her at Teddy's club', Carl said, 'where Louly worked for a while. Remember? Going by the name Kitty and serving drinks in her underwear.'

'You went up and got her,' Virgil said.

'And now she's telling marines how to fire Browning machine guns mounted in dive bombers. The guy that owns the club, Teddy Ritz, is the one told me if he ever saw me there again, I'd spend the rest of my life in a wheelchair. Teddy Ritz, the one had Shemane working in a whorehouse when she was sixteen. He was saying to her dad, you take one of my girls, I'll trade her for your daughter.'

'I don't recall what happened after,' Virgil said.

'Alvin used his influence on people he knew in Washington. They got some marshals to walk in the house with shotguns and set Shemane free.'

Virgil started to smile. 'And she didn't want to go home.'

'She liked that fast life in Kansas City. Teddy took a look at Shemane for the first time, this 16–year-old cutie, and kept her for himself. He sends a guy to Tulsa to take out Alvin. Just Alvin, but the guy empties his gun at the bed and gets both of them. This is after I went up to get Louly. I never met Shemane or heard anything about her.'

'You talk about Teddy Ritz,' Virgil said, 'you always sorta smile you mention his name.'

Carl started to smile now, sitting at the breakfast table with his coffee. 'I get a kick out of Teddy acting like a bigshot gangster.'

'Isn't that what he is?'

'Yeah, but he wants to make sure you know it.' Carl said, 'You know Tony Antonelli lives in Tulsa now? Loves it. I asked him if he knew Shemane had moved to Okmulgee. He said yeah, because he was thinking of doing a follow-up story on how she found the house for her mother since Gladys couldn't stay in Tulsa, not after her little girl became a prostitute and her husband's in bed with another one when he's shot and killed. Tony said you can't carry that kind of baggage around and still make it in Tulsa society. Then last year Shemane moved in with her mom, she said to sit back and take it easy after ten years of that life, being loaned to millionaires for out-of-town trips and popping out of cardboard birthday cakes naked. Tony said he ran into her at Deering's drugstore picking up a prescription. She said for something had been hanging on since Kansas City. I asked Tony if she meant a venereal disease. He said that's what it sounded like. He said Shemane and her mom dress for tea in the early evening, only they drink martinis and smoke reefer. I asked where she got the weed and he said Teddy Ritz, he's still taking care of her. Gives her gas stamps when she needs them. Tony says Shemane sips her martini and tells him in a soft voice what a relief it is to not have to go to bed with some guy because he was somebody. And then she'd say, "But I learned a lot from those guys. They were smart, they ran things." Tony said he changed his mind about doing a follow-up. What would it be about? Shemane and her mother putting on the dog and getting fried every night? He said it could be a funny piece but didn't want to make Shemane look pitiful. I said, "Didn't you see right away you'd be making fun of her?"

Tony said he kept going back out of curiosity. He had the feeling Shemane was up to something she didn't want anybody to know about. He said he suspected what it was but wouldn't tell me. "If it gets out, Shemane would be in serious trouble". I said, "Oh, it must be about that German POW she's been seeing".'

Carl and his dad were both grinning at each other.

Virgil said, 'You're a dirty dog.'

Carl said, 'You know how serious he takes himself?'

'That's what I'm talking about. What's he do now? Did you tell him you just took a wild guess?'

'What's wild about it? I know she's the one he's seeing. Tony said he stopped by, no one answered the bell, so he went around back and saw them in the kitchen. They were caught so she had to open the door. She called Jurgen Jim. She said Jim was a relative from out of town, stopped by on his way to the coast, but didn't say which one.'

'Stopped by in his short pants,' Virgil said.

'But never turned around so Tony didn't see PW on him anywhere. But it was the shorts in October and his haircut gave him away, Tony said he believed the guy was German, but could not say it as an absolute fact or he'd have to report it, and turn Shemane in. I said, "For what? She didn't help him escape, did she? What's she doing she'd be arrested for?"'

Virgil said, 'Giving comfort to the enemy.'

'That's what bothers Tony. I said, "Giving him comfort and maybe a dose at the same time". I told him not to worry about it, I'd talk to Shemane and find out what's going on.'

Shemane saw Carl coming up the walk and changed her mind about wearing a sweater with the slacks. She turned from the window to her closet, put on her favorite Chanel jacket, no bra, the nubby black wool, and left it unbuttoned.

The doorbell rang as she looked in on her mom across the hall, Gladys sitting in her corset at the vanity smoking a cigarette. Her mom said to the mirror, 'Somebody's at the door.' Shemane said she was getting it and went down the stairway running the fingers of both hands through her blonde hair, messing up her pageboy. The guy in the dark suit and tie, no topcoat, had got out of the Chevrolet standing in front. She didn't recognize him, but liked the way his hat sat on his head. If he wasn't from Kansas City, one of Teddy's guys, he was a local hotshot who'd heard the stories about her and had to have a look.

Shemane opened the door and watched him touch his hat before showing his marshal's star. Now he offered his card, looking her in the eye with a pleasant expression, and told her he was Carl Webster. She looked at the card that said he was Deputy United States Marshal Carlos Huntington Webster. He didn't look like a Carlos, but she liked it better than Carl. She offered her hand saying, 'I'm Shemane, Carlos. What can I do for you?'

He took her hand in both of his, feeling her fingers and rings in what she felt was an intimate way. He said, 'I hope you have time for me. I need to talk to you about something I've been wondering about.'

She knew he meant her German, but liked the way he could state his business and still show fun in his eyes. Shemane said, 'Come in, Carlos, and tell me what you'd like to drink.'

'Whatever you're having,' Carl said, following her through the dim living room, the dining room and into the kitchen, Shemane asking him if he liked martinis. Carl said he did, but had never longed for one.

Two stem glasses and a jar of olives waited on the kitchen table, a long table with a porcelain surface. It reminded him of his dad saying he had been circumsized on their porcelain kitchen table, and if he got any more famous the table might be worth something. Shemane brought a pitcher of martinis from the refrigerator and filled the glasses, saying, 'I love martinis. You know why?'

'They make you drunk?'

'They do, don't they? You get tipsy before you know it. How many olives?'

'Two,' Carl said, seeing what he could see where her jacket opened while she fished olives out of the jar.

'I like four,' Shemane said, raised her eyes to his and then her glass in a move that held the jacket open a few seconds. Carl waited until they'd both had a drink and Shemane offered him a cigarette; he struck a kitchen match with his thumbnail and she touched his hand holding the match while she got a light. He said, 'I understand you're interested in German prisoners of war.'

'Who told you?'

'Tony Antonelli. He says you drive around looking for prisoners working.'

'Once I saw a bunch of 'em marching out of a field to where the trucks are waiting, all of 'em singing away. I can't get over how much they look like Americans but are so different.'

'You can't see Americans singing like that, can you? Serious about it?'

'They're way behind the times, Germans. What I can't understand, why we're at war with them instead of helping them fight the Russians, the Bolshevik hordes. They're the bad guys.'

'Is that what Jurgen says?'

She sipped her drink and used her fingers to get one of the olives. 'You talked to him?'

'Not yet.'

'What're you gonna do, put him on bread and water for a week? What do you want me for, cooking his dinner once in a while? I don't even know how to cook. He stays a few days – nobody has any idea he's in my house – and always gives himself up.'

'The thing the Army doesn't like,' Carl said, 'it makes them look dumb.'

'They are, if they can't keep him inside.'

'What's he talk about?'

'The war.'

'He believes they're winning?'

'When we first met he did. Not anymore. He reads everything he can get his hands on, the paper, magazines ...' She smiled for the first time, a real smile. 'He read that book about you, *The Hot Kid of the Marshals Service*? Tony gave me a copy. Jurgen read it one time when he was here and asked me about you. I said he knew more than I did. He's smart, he's educated ... I went to high school two years and we argue about things. He gets what he knows from all he reads. I got mine listening to guys who know how to make money. Or, what I say sometimes, having lived as a child in a whorehouse and came out in one piece.'

Carl said, 'What do you hear from Teddy?'

She paused, 'You know Teddy or you know *of* Teddy?'

'The day we met,' Carl said, 'he had a guy hit me in the gut with a baseball bat. The next day he wanted to hire me. I know Teddy. What surprises me, he's been nice to you all this time.'

Shemane sort of shrugged. 'He can be a sweet guy.'

'He's like a father to you?'

'You're kidding, right?'

'When did Tony give you the book?'

'When it came out – Tony was writing about white slavers abducting me. Teddy loved being called a white slaver. He's read the book, says it's pretty good, very factual about Kansas City when Pendergast owned the town. Teddy keeps asking me to come up for a visit, like I've never been to Kansas City. I tell him I'm busy.'

'Doing what?'

'Taking care of Mom.'

'You tell Teddy about Jurgen?'

There was a silence. She stared at him and said after a moment, 'Why would I?'

'Brag about a guy, a German officer, escaping from a prison camp so he can be with you? Risk getting shot? What'd Teddy say, he'd like to meet him?'

'I haven't told him,' Shemane said.

Wesley Sellers was in his office waiting for Carl.

'Well, I put your boy Gary Marion in with the Kraut. I told him to leave his sidearm here and get it on the way out, and I'm glad I did. He wasn't in the cell two minutes he takes a swing at Jurgen. Jurgen grabs the folding chair Gary brought in and bangs him over the head with it. We had to run him to the hospital to get his scalp sewed up. Something like seventeen stitches.'

Carl said, 'And now Gary wants to shoot him.'

Wesley said, 'I wouldn't be surprised. Says he caught him trying to escape.'

I V

O tto Penzler's rank was SS-Sturmbannführer, or Storm Command Leader; but for the past few months, since the July 20th attempt on Hitler's life had failed, he was signing camp directives and memoranda 'Major Otto Penzler'.

Jurgen could talk to Otto. Both were from Cologne, Otto five years older and with five more years in the army, the Abwehr branch of military intelligence his first few years. Both were schooled in National Socialism and could talk the Nazi talk. Otto had joined the SS, he told Jurgen with a straight face, to be seen as an active guardian of racial purity. Jurgen said, 'Not because it's elite and you like the black uniform.' In the African desert Otto had commanded Panzers and was known among his men as the *Scharfrichter*, the Executioner of British tanks. At the Deep Fork camp he was a member of the Escape Committee.

This day in October, Otto came into the solitary confinement room with the metal folding chair the guard had given him. Jurgen, sitting on his cot, squinted in the overhead light that came on.

'I have news you won't like,' Otto said, unfolding his chair and seating himself to face Jurgen. 'But first, I have to ask why you don't come to the Committee with your escape plans. It upsets them.'

'I've told you,' Jurgen said, 'I don't make plans. I have a place where I go under the fence.'

'There's a guard you take care of?'

'I came back the first time, he asked me how I escaped. I told him I go out for a few days, that's all, I'm not actually escaping. I gave him a service medal. I give him swastika pins and arm bands, spoons, utensils from mess kits.'

Otto Penzler, who also liked to wear shorts and the soft desert cap with the long peak, brought out a pack of Camels, gave one to Jurgen and lit them. Jurgen got up from the cot to stretch and lean against the wall.

'What is the news I won't like?'

'Rommel's dead,' Otto said.

He waited for Jurgen who began to nod his head.

'They killed him,' Jurgen said.

'They made him take poison.'

'But he wasn't at Wolf's Lair?'

'Not anywhere near it. Stauffenberg arrived with the explosive device in his briefcase. He's already lost an arm and an eye for the Führer so they don't make him open the case. Huesinger was there with maps of the eastern front. Stauffenberg placed his case under the map table and excused himself, he has to make a phone call. He's outside, walking away from the conference room and the device explodes. Stauffenberg assumes the Führer is dead.'

'Why wasn't he?'

'He must have moved away from the table. Rommel was named with the ones in the plot, not as an active participant but in favor of doing away with the Führer. Rommel was Germany's favorite general – the reason he was offered poison and not hanged by the neck. If he accepted it he'd be given a state funeral and his family would be treated with honor and supported for life.'

'If he'd insisted on a trial—'

'He knew better. He'd be found guilty and his family would be on their own. We don't have to worry about it,' Otto said, 'do we? The Committee wants to know why you go out.'

'They know why.'

'They would like the woman to be German.'

'What is Morrissey, English, Irish? I know she isn't a Jew or a gypsy, or a Latin from Manhattan.'

'The only thing you do with her is go to bed?'

'The only thing being everything,' Jurgen said. 'But I'm also thinking of something, an event I'd like to see happen.'

Otto said, 'Do you know that south of McAlester, not far, is an army ammunition plant where they store bombs? The Committee wants you to blow it up. Do something for the fatherland for a change.'

'I can tell who strung up Willi Martz. You want me to?'

'Be serious for a change.'

'All right, how do I get inside the place?'

'You'll find a way.'

'Do I have to activate the bombs?'

'I said, see if blowing the place up is possible.'

'Do you remember,' Jurgen said, 'the train ride from Norfolk, Virginia to Oklahoma? How long it took, and we're still only halfway across the country? Let's say I find a way to do it. There is a tremendous explosion at this barren expanse of land in the middle of America. My only thought about it would be "So what".'

'I'll tell them you don't think it's feasible.'

'No, tell them I've been thinking about a mass escape,' Jurgen said, 'on the Führer's birthday next April. Three-hundred and sixty thousand German prisoners of war, in all the camps in America, all walk out at the same time.'

Otto waited, looking at Jurgen. 'And do what?'

'Nothing,' Jurgen said and moved his shoulders, rubbing his back against the wall. 'Or they steal cars and drive around wherever they are, honking the horns.'

'To what purpose?'

'You need a purpose? All right, first to show that we can do it,' Jurgen said. 'And second, to let them know we have a sense of humor. Americans don't think we do.'

'How do you let all the camps know about the mass escape?'

'Announce a special celebration planned for the Führer's birthday.'

'All the mail is censored,' Otto said, 'and goes through our post office at Camp Hearne in Texas. How do you tell about the escape?'

'We bring our people at the post office into the plan,' Jurgen said. 'They know how to slip notes into letters already passed by the censor.'

They smoked their cigarettes and were quiet until Jurgen said, 'Why don't you come out with me sometime? I remember your girlfriend in Benghazi, the very pretty blonde Italian? I'm thinking Shemane could fix you up.'

'The time they finally get tired of looking stupid and shoot you,' Otto said, 'is the time I happen to be with you.'

Last night after seeing Shemane, Carl went back to his dad's house. He told Virgil about Gary Marion, the one who wanted to be the new hot kid, how he took a swing at Jurgen and Jurgen laid him out with a chair.

'Gary wants to be like you,' Virgil said, 'but didn't have your upbringing, learning the finer points of being a man.'

They were in the kitchen so Carl used the phone there to give the operator the number.

Virgil said to Narcissa at the stove, the woman stirring tomato sauce in an iron pot, 'He's calling Kansas City.'

'Ask him he wants to stay. We having his favorite.'

'I think he's moved back,' Virgil said, 'so he can call long distance and it won't cost him nothing.'

'Who is he calling this time?'

Carl said, 'I want to speak to Teddy. Tell him Deputy US Marshal Carlos Webster is waiting but won't wait too long. Understand?'

Virgil said to Narcissa, 'He wants to talk to that gangster, Teddy Ritz. Louly said the waitresses at his club had to wear teddies, that's all, and high heels.'

Carl said into the phone, 'Teddy? ... Yeah, it's been a while. I hear you got thrown out of your job. It's what happens the guy you're working for goes to prison.'

Virgil said to Narcissa, 'You remember Pendergast? Ran Kansas City wide open till the serious people got down on him.'

Saying this while Teddy was telling Carl not to worry about him, his club was the hottest spot in town, wall-to-wall GIs.

Carl said, 'I hear you're still being nice to Shemane,' and waited while Teddy decided what to tell him.

'Shemane,' Teddy said, 'I can talk to Shemane and know she's listening and gets what I'm telling her ... besides being the best ten minutes in bed I've ever had in my life. You been talking to her?'

'I had to question her about a German POW she's seeing.'

'She visits this guy?'

'He busts out and visits her. Spends a couple of days at her house and gives himself up. Jurgen Schrenk. She must've told you about him.'

'He gives himself up,' Teddy said. 'Then what?'

'They put him in solitary for a week, but it doesn't stop him from busting out. Four times this year.'

'What's Shemane do for him?'

'What do you think? She comforts him.'

'Couldn't she get locked up for that?'

'I'm not after Shemane, I want to find out what this Nazi's up to,' Carl said, making Jurgen a Nazi to get Teddy's reaction.

'One of the bad guys, uh?'

'He's Afrika Korps, those guys grew up Nazis. They want you to know they're tough as nails and the only reason they surrendered, their tanks ran out of gas. This Jurgen can't sit still. I keep expecting him to start blowing up oil wells or setting fire to storage tanks. I mean for the hell of it, something to do.'

'Impress Shemane,' Teddy said, 'get her excited.'

'She thinks he's a nice guy. She says we ought to be helping the Germans fight the Bolsheviks.'

'Jurgen fed her that?'

'She needs somebody to tell her what's going on over there, the Nazis trying to get rid of the Jews, sending them to slave-labor camps. I imagine you have people over there seeing it first-hand.'

Virgil said to Narcissa, 'You know Teddy's Jewish.'

He looked over to see Carl nodding his head, listening to Teddy for several minutes before saying, 'Come on – you believe that? How do you know it's true?' He listened again and said, 'What's the guy's name, Zigmund? I wish you'd let Shemane know about it – you say she pays attention to what you tell her. Give her a call and set her straight. She could help me find out what Jurgen's up to.'

He hung up and looked over to see Virgil and Narcissa watching him.

'Teddy says last year a million-and-a-half Jews in Poland disappeared.'

The light came on as Carl entered the solitary confinement room. He unfolded the chair saying, 'This is the one you hit him with?' and sat down.

Jurgen pushed up from the cot. 'The same kind.'

'What did you say made him take a swing at you?'

'Nothing. He wanted to fight,' Jurgen said. 'He walked in saying, "You don't tell me where you go, I'm gonna beat the snot out of you". Is that a popular American expression now, to beat the snot out of someone?'

'What did you say to him?'

'I told him where I go is none of his business. He kept referring to us as Krauts. "You Krauts act like you're on vacation here. You Krauts act like you're better than us." I said, "Maybe we are".' He said, "You think you can take me?" and came toward me with the chair in front of him, folded, holding it in both hands. He pushed the chair at me, let go of it to swing at my face, but now I had the chair. I raised it as he threw his punch and his fist hit the metal seat. I raised it higher and brought it down on his head. I hit him with it again as he fell to the floor.'

'Gary said you were waiting for him and took him by surprise,' Carl said. 'You grabbed the chair out of his hands and hit him with it.'

'You believe what this fellow tells you,' Jurgen said, 'or you believe me?'

'It doesn't matter,' Carl said. 'Gary's the good guy and you're the enemy. He asked you to tell him where you go when you slip out—'

'Or he'll beat the snot out of me. Is that a serious threat, Carl? He'll hit me until der Schleim comes out of my nose?'

'We're all curious about where you go,' Carl said, 'so I looked into it. I find out you spend your time with Miss Shemane Morrissey, former Kansas City call girl they say charged two hundred dollars to spend the night with her. Tell me how you first got together.'

'You've talked to her?'

'Yes, I have.'

'Well, I was walking along the road, she stopped her car. What difference does it make? I'm seeing her,' Jurgen said, 'and you know I am, so there is no mystery. You want to shock me, say she was a prostitute – I know that. She told me everything, how a white slaver by the name of Teddy Ritz put her to work before he even saw her. Then when he did – she's sixteen, very attractive – she became his mistress.' Jurgen seemed to smile saying, 'Teddy Ritz, the white slaver who must be a Jew. It's good, isn't it, the story of her life? She told me she could make a thousand dollars a week without breathing hard.'

Carl saw her making 50,000 a year with two weeks off. If she took a month off she'd still make 48,000.

'What I want to know,' Jurgen said, 'is why you call me a Kraut?'

'We call all of you Krauts. It caught on and it's how you're known. Short for sauerkraut.'

'Yes . . . ?'

'Isn't it your national dish?'

'I'm not sure,' Jurgen said, and asked Carl, 'Do you like sauerkraut?'

'I'll eat it if it's what we're having.'

'I eat it, I'm a Kraut,' Jurgen said. 'You eat it, you remain who you are.'

'It doesn't have to make sense,' Carl said. 'The *Tulsa World*, and my dad call you Huns most of the time. You mind "Huns"?'

'No, it's Kraut I don't care for.'

'Don't worry about it,' Carl said. 'What I want you to tell me is how the hard-nosed Nazis have come to run the camps. Because they're mean buggers but disciplined, they do what they're told? That's why the guards prefer Nazis. Tell me why they intimidate the less Nazified ones; beat them up, go so far as to lynch them, the ones you call suicides? I want to hear what you have to say about Nazis, and tell me what they did with a million-and-a-half Jews in Poland.'

'A million-and-a-half,' Jurgen said. 'I thought it was more like three million have gone missing. The Russians have accounted for half of them.'

V

'You see us,' Jurgen said to Carl Webster in the solitary confinement room, 'we are either Nazis or we're against them. You don't see degrees of belief between the two extremes?'

'You know how to sound like a Nazi,' Carl said, 'to get by in the camp, you and your friend Otto Penzler, going back to when you were Hitler Jugend and learned the spiel. Otto makes sure you know he's SS, an elite group of thugs as Nazified as you can get. But I can't see either of you guys wanting to live in a police state. People telling on each other. Kids telling on their mom and dad. People hearing the truck coming and know it's the SS on a roundup. And you think, Oh, my God, in the beerhall last night you said if that fat slob Goering and that gimp Goebbels and that humorless twit Himmler, if those guys represent the master race . . . You don't remember what else you said but that would be enough. How many people are tried and hanged for making remarks like that? They torture you, pull out your fingernails . . . You go along with that? You look up to Hitler as an inspiring leader?'

'As leaders go,' Jurgen said, smoking one of Carl's Chesterfields, 'he hasn't done too badly. He made himself Führer in 'thirty-four. He restored the German Reich. By 1942 he owned Norway, Denmark, Belgium, Luxembourg, Yugoslavia – I forget Holland – also Greece, Czechoslovakia, Poland and a big chunk of Russia and the Ukraine.' Jurgen paused to draw on his cigarette. 'Still, Erwin Rommel, after North Africa when he was appointed to the Führer's staff, and personally witnessed the Führer's outbursts and irrational behavior, he told people close to him the Führer was over the edge, far from normal. I was with Rommel most of two years,' Jurgen said, 'and believe every word he ever said to me and continued to believe him, his predictions, his assessments of the war, even when they failed to happen. He is the only man I have ever known I would step in front of to take a bullet meant for him.'

'For Rommel,' Carl said, 'but not your Führer?'

'I would be happy to see someone kill him,' Jurgen said, 'if he doesn't do it himself.'

'The YMCA gives you radios,' Carl said, 'and you modify them to receive shortwave broadcasts from Germany. You need parts, you order them from a Sears and Roebuck catalog. The camp commander says they find shortwave radios that were meant to be found, but you have other transmitters and receivers hidden away.'

'You want me to tell you,' Jurgen said, 'if I know where they are?'

'I want to know,' Carl said, 'if you believe what the broadcasts from home tell you. We listen to them. They get finished playing a big military number, they report that your guys are bravely holding the line "with heroic efforts". You believe that's true?'

'I believe we're resisting bravely, yes. What else can we do?'

'Shemane said you've stopped talking about winning the war. What about most of your guys? Are they still optimistic?'

'Many of them, yes. Or they would have to believe in Anglo-American victories, what they read in your newspapers. I'll tell you something,' Jurgen said, 'coming here, crossing this country that can take days, seeing all the lights in the cities we pass, seeing no evidence of destruction from bombing raids, it gives us doubts about what we were told, that industrial cities were bombed, and of course New York City. But our comrades who came through New York saw little or no damage from bombs.'

'They didn't see any,' Carl said. 'You have bombers that can fly across the Atlantic Ocean, drop their loads, turn around and fly back to Europe?'

'They would have to refuel.'

'Where? Where do you stop for gas over here?'

Jurgen didn't answer. He took his time to say, 'You want to know about the Jewish Question.'

'The first thing he did when he took power,' Jurgen said, 'was dismiss all Jews working in civil service. He also began to reduce their numbers in the various professions. The Führer saw no Jews as workers in factories or the trades like carpenters. He saw them as a race of merchants and money lenders, and called them our deadliest enemy.'

'German people,' Carl said, 'who happened to be Jews.'

'Blaming them for whatever was wrong with Germany,' Jurgen said. 'The Führer passed the Nuremburg Laws, the idea, to unite all Germans and exclude the Jews as citizens. For a German to marry a Jew was forbidden. Jews were no longer permitted to practice law or medicine except among themselves, but if you were part Jewish you could be a pharmacist. Are you following this? Jews were prohibited from attending German theaters, concerts, film houses. They could no longer attend German schools. They were forbidden to own firearms. In fact, the day before Kristallnacht in November, 1938, the SS went into Jewish homes and removed anything that could be used as a weapon. You know about Kristallnacht, the night of broken glass?'

'When they started wrecking Jewish stores, places of business,' Carl said. 'I remember seeing it on the newsreel. The cops watching the brown shirts smashing shop windows.'

'They burned synagogues,' Jurgen said, 'all over Germany. They destroyed thousands of shops, businesses. Some of the Jews were killed and as many as 30,000 arrested and sent to labor camps. This was the beginning of violence against the Jews, 1938. I asked my father if he believed this kind of persecution was going on. I said, "Can you believe our government is systematically killing people it doesn't like?" I asked him this while we were in Detroit and were reading about it in the paper. My father said, "Give the impression you accept National Socialism, since you have no other choice, and never in a public place criticize our Führer or any of the lunatics working for him". My father was a production engineer with Ford of Germany, or Ford Werke, as it was called. A year after we left Detroit and came home, the Führer awarded Henry Ford, on his seventy-fifth birthday, the Grand Cross of the German Eagle, the highest honor we give someone who isn't German.'

'I did read that Hitler had a portrait of Ford on his office wall in Munich. Your dad said to give the impression that you accept National Socialism?'

'He didn't mean act like a Nazi. Act like you believe in the future of the Third Reich and you don't mind being a member of the master race. He said it isn't something we have to deal with directly.'

'Don't think about it,' Carl said, 'it might go away.'

'You have the same kind of problem,' Jurgen said, 'in the way you treat Negroes – American citizens, but black. I'm in the café waiting to be picked up. Let's say two Negro GIs come in pointing carbines at me, playing, pretending I'm a desperate character.'

Carl listened, knowing what Jurgen was going to say.

'I sit at the counter, the enemy, the Kraut, having my coffee, having whatever I want. But the two guys in uniform can't sit at the counter with me. They aren't allowed to because of their race.'

'I think they could sit at that counter if they wanted,' Carl said.

'But not at every counter in America, or use the drinking fountain and toilets reserved for whites,' Jurgen said. 'You know what I'm talking about.'

Nazis and redneck racists were not the same in Carl's mind and he could argue the difference with Jurgen. But not today.

'I have to leave you,' Carl said, 'get back to Tulsa to pick up my wife.'

'I don't think you ever said you were married. You have children?'

'Not yet,' Carl said. 'We're waiting till she gets out of the Marines.'

Jurgen gave him a funny look.

Carl said, 'Yeah, what?'

He was so glad to see Louly coming along the station platform in her uniform, he ran up, got his arms around her and they started kissing, both of them holding on to each other until Carl's hat came off and he let it go. When they parted for a breath, Louly said, 'You remember the time in Kansas City, we were in the car kissing away and I knocked your hat off? Not all the way off but cockeyed, and right away you had to take it off, knowing you didn't look like a cool customer the way it sat on your head? You remember that?'

Carl said, 'I wasn't gonna take it off this time till we got out of bed.'

'You know how long from now that'll be if we're going to your dad's house? He'll ask me about the Woman Marines, but I don't get to answer. It reminds him of women insurrectionists who fought alongside the Mambis in Cuba, and there were some he knew and had camped with, while I'm trying to look interested.'

'We're staying here,' Carl said. 'I used my influence and got us a suite at the Mayo for as long as we want.'

She said, 'You really love me, don't you?' The two of them lying around the hotel suite in their underwear, drinking bourbon highballs, ordering club sandwiches and potato chips from room service, smoking cigarettes, taking baths together worn out from making love, Louly lying back between his legs in the bubblebath, her head resting on his chest, telling Carl about teaching flexible gunnery to Marine radiomen who would sit behind the pilot in an SBD Dauntless dive bomber, ready to shoot down Zekes that got after them without shooting off their own tail.

Carl said, 'If I was in your class, I'd see you as that redheaded big-ass Marine who looks lonely.'

'Anybody tries to get close, I tell him I've shot two men with two different revolvers. One, to save the life of the man I knew I would marry. For the other I was given $500 by a bankers association for shooting a bank robber in a tourist court where he was holding me against my will. Deputy Marshal Carlos Webster said stay with that and you won't go to jail. Remember?'

'I remember your big brown eyes looking up at me.'

'But it wasn't till you came to Kansas City I knew for sure you loved me. When I was going by Kitty.'

'Working for Teddy,' Carl said. 'I spoke to him on the phone yesterday about Shemane. You don't remember her?'

'I told you,' Louly said, 'I'd only heard about her. How Teddy had her kidnapped and put in a whorehouse 'cause her dad got one of Teddy's girls to move to Tulsa.' Louly stopped and said, 'This could be the same suite they were in, when Teddy's guy shot them.'

'They were up on nine,' Carl said. 'Teddy liked Shemane a lot, didn't he?'

'He liked girls,' Louly said. 'I wouldn't mind seeing him again.'

'What for?'

'In my uniform. Ask him what he's doing for the war effort these days, besides getting GIs drunk.'

Carl said, 'I thought he knew about Shemane entertaining her German POW, but she hadn't told him. I said to Teddy he ought to let her know what they're doing to the Jews. She thinks they're all nice guys from good homes.'

Louly said, 'That's right, Teddy's Jewish.'

'And he's got relatives over in Poland who've disappeared. He hears from a cousin named Zigmund he calls Ziggy. Ziggy used to smuggle food into the Warsaw ghetto. All the Jews were kept inside the walls ten to twenty feet high. Ziggy said the Germans'd go inside the ghetto and do whatever they want. One time they brought out sixty prominent Jews everyone knew and respected and shot them in the street. Now they're bringing out five or six thousand at a time and sending them to a concentration camp only forty miles away, called Treblinka. They arrive, some are put to work and the rest are sent to a gas chamber. In a few minutes they're dead and the bodies are burned in a crematorium.'

Louly said, 'A crema*tori*um?' She got around sideways between

Carl's legs in the bubblebath to stare at his face. 'You believe that?'

'Ziggy told Teddy it's been going on for a few years. Some are put to work digging pits, long ones like ditches, only much deeper. Men, women and children are brought out and machine-gunned. They fall in the pit and the bodies are covered with lime.'

Louly was facing Carl now, sitting back on her hands holding on to the sides of the tub.

'Thousands of people are murdered and we don't hear anything about it?'

'Ziggy told Teddy almost all the Jews who were living in Poland have disappeared.'

'They're dead?'

'Shot or gassed, those that haven't starved to death.'

'Ziggy saw it happen?'

'Or heard about it from people who did.'

Louly was shaking her head. 'I don't believe it.'

'Jurgen admits it. He says the POWs that hear about it don't want to believe it either. They can't see soldiers like themselves killing women and children. Jurgen said it's the SS doing it, not soldiers. The boss, Bob McMahon, said they know about it in Washington, the Nazis bent on exterminating an entire people. That's the word Washington uses, exterminate. You can read about Nazi atrocities in the paper, but they aren't played up because they're too hard to believe. So the papers focus on how we're beating up on the Japanese.'

'How about the one that shot you,' Louly said, 'who wasn't supposed to be there?'

'I told you, I was hit right here,' Carl said, turning in the bubblebath to pinch the slight bulge above his left hip, 'and in the leg. Broke the bone.'

'What happened to the guy?'

'The Nip? There were two of them. Listen, I'm going to make

us highballs, order up some mixed nuts. You want anything?'

'You won't talk about it,' Louly said. 'Why?'

'Are you kidding? I tell everybody,' Carl said. 'Come on, let's have a drink.'

'You don't want to admit some guy got the drop on you.'

'Honey, this is different, it's a war story. Get dry and I'll tell you what happened.'

VI

C arl was shaving in his white undershorts in the bathroom, the door open, his highball on the counter; he'd come out to the bedroom to stand over Louly at the vanity in a peach teddy, brushing snags out of her red hair, Carl stooping to shave in the vanity mirror while he told Louly his war story.

How they lived in Quonset huts on Momote plantation among rows of coconut palms, the 5000–foot air strip cutting a wide swatch of packed coral through the trees. He told her fighter planes took off every day – Australians in Hurricanes and Spitfires, the Navy sending F4Us and Hellcats – to drop bombs on by-passed Japanese bases like Rabaul, keeping a good 100,000 Nips out of the war.

'Did you eat much coconut?'

'Hardly any.'

'Why not?'

'Too much trouble, and the milk gives you the runs. We hung mosquito netting over our bunks and took Atabrine tablets every day. It could turn your skin yellow.'

'So you didn't take any.'

'Once in a while I did.'

'How was the chow?' The marine sounding interested.

'Poor to not too bad, but I ate it. Most of the time, we wore greens, the shirts and pants,' Carl said, stepping into the bathroom to hold his razor under the faucet and drink some of his highball, 'and green baseball caps, or you could wear your white cover. You could wear dungarees or just about anything you wanted, Seabees weren't that military. We'd cut the pants down to shorts and the sleeves off the shirts, cut our combat boots into sandals.'

'It must've been *hot*,' Louly said, making a face, her brush caught in a snag.

Carl took the brush, worked it free and put it back in her hand saying, 'Two degrees from the equator, you sweet little thing, you know it was hot. But we always had a breeze off the Bismarck Sea. I can't tell you where the sea ends and it becomes the Pacific Ocean again. I asked Jurgen – he's the one told me why it's the Bismarck Sea, Germany taking over the Admiralties in 1885 and owned them up to World War One. I said to Jurgen I was surprised you didn't put up any statues, Bismarck or any of your Kraut heroes like the Kaiser. I think Australia owns the islands now. Manus, the big one, has a huge harbor, so they made it Seventh Fleet headquarters. Los Negros is only ten miles long, but curves around close to Manus and forms one side of the harbor. We were issued a carbine and three magazines of ammo, forty-five rounds. And I had my .38 along.'

'You brought it with you?' Louly surprised.

'I wore it every day for fifteen years. It felt good the time I packed it.'

Louly paused, holding the hair brush in the air.

'You never told me what your job was.'

'The lieutenant would tell me to get in the jeep and go check on something. We had a lot of heavy equipment working, bulldozers and graders.' Carl smiled at himself in the vanity mirror, half turned and made a muscle for Louly. 'You like my tattoo?'

'I love it.' She said, 'It's Palmer Method, huh?' looking at "Carlos" on his shoulder, in perfect penmanship.

'Only cost me a buck.'

He reached around Louly to get a towel off the vanity. He wiped his face and said, 'Look up here.' Louly looked straight up at him bending her head back and he kissed her till she reached up and took his face in her hands.

After that tender moment he said, 'They gave us the carbine and a steel helmet. Once in a while they'd announce General Quarters over the PA and we'd go down to the beach and wait for something to happen. The thing the helmet was good for, it held two cans of beer in chipped ice we'd each take to the show at night. We're Seabees, so we made seats with arms and a back that would hook on to the plank nailed to a log – rows of hard boards going back from the screen. It rained it didn't matter, we'd go to the show. One night I was with this young Seabee, George Klein from Chicago, in the rain watching Lauren Bacall in her first movie, *To Have and Have Not* where she tells Humphrey Bogart if he wants anything just whistle? Lauren Bacall says to him, "You know how to whistle, Steve. You put your lips together and blow." And George Klein went crazy. At that moment he fell in love with Lauren Bacall and kept saying, "We're the same age. You know it? Look at her. Lauren Bacall and I are the exact same age."'

'How'd he know that?'

'I don't know, but you could see she was a kid. Listen, the guy working the projector – I made him put the same reel back on as he was changing reels so we could watch her say it again. Sitting in the rain.'

Louly said, 'Are you coming to where you got shot? I think you said in the letter you were in a boat?'

'It was called a Duck,' Carl said, 'it was green and looks like a thirty-foot open boat but has wheels. You drive out of the water and keep going. We'd take it across a stream separating us from Manus, Los Negros was that close, and go to the supply depot for stores and sixty cases of beer. All the cans olive drab, it didn't matter what kind. On our base we kept them in a walk-in cooler and handed out two or three cans per man every other day. Naval Air Transport pilots always had whiskey and they'd sell it for thirty-five to fifty bucks a fifth if they needed money. Or sometimes they'd trade a bottle for a case of beer.'

'You were in the Duck,' Louly said, 'when you got shot . . .'

Carl was in the bathroom rinsing, now drying his face. He said, 'We were coming back from Manus with our stores. Crossed the stream to Los Negros, up the bank and into some growth, and the Nip hit me with a rifle shot.' Carl stepped into the bedroom pinching the love handle above his left hip. 'George Klein was with me and a big boy from Arkansas named Elmer Whaley. I remember he and I sucking on Beachnut scrap that trip. There were more shots as I dove for cover in the stern and saw George and Elmer Whaley go down. Not shot, taking cover. I listened to that rifle fire again in my head and held up two fingers to my mates. I said, "We don't know where they are. We have to wait till they come to us." I said, "You're dead, so don't move". George said they didn't have their carbines. I didn't have mine either.'

Louly said, 'You go armed cause something like this could happen—'

'No,' Carl said, 'the island was secured. The First Cavalry swore, no live Japs left. Over three thousand killed. The First Cavalry lost something like three hundred killed and eleven hundred wounded. The war on Los Negros was over. No, we brought the carbines for fun, fire off a few rounds.'

'Where were they, the guns?'

'Up front, at the bow. George was crawling toward them.'

'By then you must've had your .38 in your hand,' Louly said. 'The one with the front sight filed off?'

'I believe it was,' Carl said, starting to grin.

'The same one I used the time I saved my husband's life?'

Carl was grinning at her in the vanity mirror.

'You have the hammer eared back?'

'I believe I did.'

'You hear them coming through the growth?'

'Taking forever. They're both off to the left, so I held the .38 on the port-side gunnel where I thought they'd appear, judging from the noise they're making coming through the growth. I see an oriental face in a dirty cap appear above the gunnel – he's bringing up his rifle as I shot him. Now the other one, taller than the first guy, appears and I see him aiming at me as I'm looking right at him, his face pressed against the stock of his rifle. I shot him a half second before he fired and it threw him off. I got hit in the leg instead of between the eyes.'

'My hero,' Louly said, head lowered to brush her hair, her eyes raised to Carl in the mirror. 'I remember you got your medals and your honorable discharge and quit limping.'

'I'd served my country,' Carl said.

'And I'm just starting.' Louly quit brushing. 'Tomorrow I'm the lady marine at a war bond rally.'

'What do you do?'

'Smile, act cute in a military kind of way. Roy Eldridge and Anita O'Day'll be there, and some others.'

'"Let Me Off Uptown,"' Carl said. 'Roy and Anita don't need any others. I'll try to make it, but first I have to supervise a new guy, Gary Marion. You want to picture him, he's one of those tough little bullriders from the rodeo.'

'What's wrong with him?'

'I have to settle him down before he starts shooting Germans.'

There was a coalminer named Joe Tanzi from Krebs, who started digging coal when he was a kid, 13 years old but big for his age. On his 44th birthday, still going down in the mines, he told his wife he wasn't going to work anymore. He was going to hitch a ride to McAlester and rob the first bank he came to on Choctaw Avenue. Two weeks before this, at Osage No. 5, an explosion sealed off Joe Tanzi for four days with four dead miners and five lunch pails. Joe didn't eat much, the smell of the dead miners made him sick. He decided he was through with mines.

His kids were grown by then. The boys had left Krebs for Tulsa and the oil fields, and the girls were married and keeping house. His wife locked the front door and went to her mother's.

That morning Joe Tanzi had put on a clean shirt and pants with his wornout suitcoat, his cap, hitched the ride to McAlester and walked in the bank. He took out a pistol he'd bought for six dollars off an old guy who was supposed to have been a Black Hand assassin in his time, and robbed the bank of 7,700 dollars of miners' payroll.

What he did then, he got on the interurban streetcar and rode it twenty miles to Hartshorne, the end of the line, where he was arrested the next morning at the home of his oldest sister, Loretta, who was known as Grandma Tanzi and made a living brewing and selling Choc beer to coalminers. They asked Joe Tanzi, all right, where was the money? Joe Tanzi, one of those big guys who didn't talk much, said, 'What money?'

They had bank people identify him and a hundred witnesses who saw him riding the streetcar with bank sacks. They asked him where he'd hid it. He wouldn't answer. They asked him using blackjacks on his kidneys till he was peeing blood and he still wouldn't tell them. For several days they searched his sister's house, her car, her property and adjoining lots. They brought dogs to the sister's house to sniff out in all directions. Once they gave up, knowing he'd never speak a word to them, they brought Joe Tanzi to federal court, charged him with bank robbery, found him guilty in five minutes and, mad as hell, sentenced him to twenty-five years of hard labor. This was in 1928.

In 1933 Joe Tanzi was one of six convicts in a work crew repaving Stonewall Avenue from McAlester's business district to the prison. He heard the signal as they were coming to the Barnett Memorial Church, a wolf whistle, and the six convicts took off in all directions. Joe Tanzi ran for the church, hearing gunfire from the guards, but none of it coming at him. He got around back of the church and inside, the door unlocked, a man in there playing the organ, booming through part of a hymn when he heard the gunfire, went to a window to see what was going on. It allowed Joe Tanzi to get behind the organ in time to hear the guards coming, shouting, and heard the organist tell them nobody came in here, he'd of seen them. That night Joe Tanzi got pants and a shirt still damp off a clothesline, burned his prison stripes and walked two full nights to Hartshorne and dug up his bank money buried six feet deep in the middle of Grandma Tanzi's cornfield. The two thought they ought to move to Arkansas and that's what they did: paid 900 dollars for a dinky farm near Mulberry, on the road east of Fort Smith.

'I guess they missed living in Oklahoma,' Carl said to Gary Marion, ''cause now they have a farm near Idabel, close to the Red River. Cross it you're in Texas.'

They were riding in the '41 Chevrolet sedan with 180,000 miles on it but good tires, Gary driving, Carl watching the ex-bullrider staring straight ahead at the highway. 'You start to see a lot more dogwoods you know you're coming to Idabel.'

Gary said, 'This convict'll be armed?'

'I don't know. He might be.'

'He robbed the bank he was armed.'

'Sixteen years ago,' Carl said. 'You want him still holding a gun, don't you?'

Earlier in this trip, talking about Jurgen Schrenk, Gary maintained POWs were no better than fugitive offenders. He said he walked in that cell and Jurgen was set on killing him. 'Why would he care about you?' Carl said. 'Jurgen's a combat veteran, a captain in the Afrika Korps. He doesn't even have to talk to you he doesn't want to. What we'll do is forget the whole thing.'

Approaching Idabel, Carl said, 'There are fugitive felons we can't wait to find, and there are guys like Joe Tanzi who dug coal till he couldn't dig any more. Some parolee around here recognized him from prison and went to the county sheriff. Who knows why? Joe Tanzi's a federal fugitive, so the sheriff called Tulsa. Joe's sixty years old now, his sister's about eighty. They say he bought a full section off a Choctaw was trying to grow cotton. Joe's letting a colored family sharecrop it with him.'

'But he still owes us twenty years,' Gary said. 'Commit the crime, you do the time.'

Carl could hear himself saying that when he was 25. But even back then he wasn't anything like Gary Marion, Jesus, from some dinky town in east Texas.

'We'll visit Joe and have a talk.'

'What about?'

'See what he's calling himself.' Carl stopped and said, 'When you were competing for rodeo money you had to stay on the bull eight seconds, right? You don't get any points for staying on longer, you're judged on your ride. You hear the buzzer you try to slide off without getting thrown. Then you want to walk to the gate without looking back, see what the bull's doing. Am I right?'

'There's girls in the stands watching,' Gary said. 'You take your hat off to them and keep turning to wave it at the entire arena.'

'While you're checking on the bull.'

'Some you better.'

'It doesn't mean you're afraid of the bull.'

'No – you're showing him respect is all.'

'It's the same kind of thing,' Carl said, 'you're a peace officer. You try to handle the bull and make it look easy.'

Gary turned his head to point his old-timer Stetson at Carl. 'What I think you're saying to me, leave the guinea convict to grow his cotton and nobody gets hurt.'

Carl said, 'Gary, you wear me out. I'm not sure why, but you and I don't seem to communicate. What I get from the way you see this, you hope Joe Tanzi pulls a gun so you can shoot him.'

'He pulls,' Gary said, 'isn't that what you're supposed to do?'

VII

S outh of Idabel they came to the crossroads Carl was looking
for, a sheriff's car waiting by a patch of dogwoods. It was
late in the day but still light for another hour or so.

Two McCurtain County deputies came to Carl's side of the
car and he got out to meet them and show his star. Gary
Marion watched, still in the car, his hands hanging on the
steering wheel. He noticed that the deputies seemed to defer
to Carl, waiting for him to speak, ask them questions. One of
the deputies said the man identified as Joe Tanzi hadn't left his
property, down that way toward the river. He asked if Carl
wanted them along for backup. Carl said he didn't want to
alarm the man, put him on his guard, anymore than he had
to; he thought he and Gary – Carl turning to glance at him in
the car – should be able to handle this one. He said, 'You
check the name on the deed?'

'Joseph Shikoba,' the deputy said. 'According to his story,
related to the Choctaw sold him the farm.'

'But this convict on parole,' Carl said, 'says he's Joe Tanzi. Why you suppose the con wants to send Joe back to prison? If we find out it is Joe Tanzi?'

The deputy said, 'It don't sound like they were friends inside, does it?'

'How big a boy is Joseph?'

'Big. Has a good hundred pounds on you.'

Gary Marion listened and wasn't going to say another word to Carl getting in the car, Carl telling him to go left down the road, it was only a couple miles now. But Gary couldn't keep quiet.

'You don't believe this guy is Joe Tanzi?'

'I'll talk to him and find out who he is,' Carl said, 'to my satisfaction.'

'The con swore he's Joe Tanzi. He knew him five years inside the Walls.

Carl said, 'Why does my wanting to give this man some slack upset you?'

Was he kidding?

Because Gary had read the book about the hot kid of the marshals service, joined up and couldn't wait to shake hands with Carlos Huntington Webster, who packed a Colt .38 on a .45 frame, the front sight filed off. Only this Carl Webster, back from the war in the Pacific, wasn't anything like the Carl Webster in the book.

Gary said, 'You shot and killed one armed offender after another, starting with the cow thief you blew out of his saddle when you were fifteen years old. You joined the marshals and went after Emmett Long, the deadliest bank robber of the Twenties, faced him in a farmhouse near Checotah, warned him if you pulled you'd shoot to kill, and you did. There was the time you faced David Lee Swick coming out of the bank in Turley, firing at you while holding a woman in front of him. You pulled and shot what you saw of him from twenty feet.'

Carl said, 'You know the woman fainted? For a minute I was afraid I'd shot her.' He looked at the gravel road and said, 'Pull up here for a minute.'

Gary eased to a stop, not yet finished with what he was saying. 'According to your book you shot Peyton Bragg at four hundred yards with a Winchester. At night, Peyton running from your posse.'

Carl said, 'You remember reading about the woman Peyton was seeing, Venicia Munson?'

Gary didn't answer, he had another one to tell.

'You shot the four guys who drove their car into the roadhouse that time, all of them coming out armed and standing fairly close. One of 'em, Nester Lott, the ex-federal agent gone bad, packed two .45s cinched to his legs. Nestor pulled on you and you shot him and turned and shot the other three.' Gary paused.

Carl said, 'This friend of Peyton's, Venicia Munson, was an old-maid school teacher who drank Peyton's wildcat whiskey and didn't care who knew it. We're sitting in her kitchen waiting for Peyton to show, she told me she was scared to death. I said, "Well, that'll teach you to get mixed up with a bank robber". She said, "You're the one scares me, not Peyton. I can tell you'd rather shoot him than bring him in," She said it was why I became a marshal, to get to carry a gun and shoot people.'

For a few moments there it was quiet in the car, Gary frowning, anxious to say something, Carl waiting for him to think of the words, Gary looking out the window now as he said, 'You listen to a woman doesn't know what she's talking about?'

'Except while I'm sitting there with her,' Carl said, 'I'm thinking I had a chance of adding Peyton Bragg to my list. At that time he'd be number four.'

'I can understand that,' Gary said, nodding his head.

'When I was younger,' Carl said, 'I'd see movies like *Ace of Aces* and bite my fingernails watching Richard Dix flying a Spad or a Camel and shooting down Germans. You knew they were evil by the strange kind of goggles they wore and how they always looked arrogant. Richard Dix would get on the tail of a three-winged Fokker, give it a burst and salute the Kraut spiraling down trailing smoke. They'd add another German cross to his plane, under the cockpit. At one time, when I first became a marshal, I thought, they go up looking for enemy planes to shoot down and we go out to take wanted felons dead or alive.'

Gary was nodding again.

'But their dogfights and our gunfights,' Carl said, 'aren't near the same. Theirs are aerial shows, graceful, their planes looping around in the clouds, killing from a distance, spinning down in slow circles with that trail of smoke. Ours, we get to see the ones we kill, dead eyes staring at us, blood staining the pavement. People shot to death aren't pretty, are they?' Carl took his time to say, 'How many felons have you seen killed by law officers?'

'Well, not any,' Gary said, 'just yet. But I've seen people killed in car wrecks and they're an awful sight.'

They drove up to the farmhouse worn, bare and rickety by sun and Oklahoma dust, a new washing machine on the porch. Now a man came out to stand with his hand resting on the washer. He was a size, more than six feet to see him there. Still in the car Carl said, 'You see the old woman?' Gary, staring at the house, shook his head. Carl said, 'Look at the window. Those are the double ought holes of a shotgun parting the curtains. And I'm gonna guess there's a gun in that washing machine. That's how much they want to stay here and grow cotton. We get out, don't say a word. You got that?'

Gary mumbled something.

'Have you got that?'

'I said yeah.'

They came out now to stand on each side of the car's headlights. Carl identified himself and Gary to the man on the porch, who hadn't said a word or taken his hand from the washing machine.

'You're Joseph Shikoba?'

The man nodded and said, 'What do you want?'

'You bought this property—'

'From a man related to one of my uncles.'

'You're Choctaw.'

'Part of me.'

'Where you from?'

'Here. All my life.'

'You planted yet?'

The man shifted from one foot to the other. 'Now is too late. Next year we gonna have cotton and the year after that, every year we gonna grow cotton.'

'I'll tell the sheriff,' Carl said, 'you're not the man we're looking for. I'm sorry we bothered you.'

In the car again, turned around heading north, Gary said, 'I don't get it. We could have him in the back seat, cuffed.'

'You'd have to kill his sister.'

'All right, what do you tell McMahon?

'We couldn't find him.'

'He'll believe you?'

'Bob will call the sheriff and the sheriff will threaten to jail the snitch for making a false accusation.'

'All right, let me ask you something,' Gary looking from the road to Carl. You said you made up your mind to add Peyton to your list. You gave him a number, he'd be number four at that time. He's close to getting away, pretty far down the road when you shot him.'

'What's the question?'

'Why didn't you let him go? You're letting Joe Tanzi off the hook when he ought to be in prison. Why didn't you give Peyton a break, let him get away?'

'Joe Tanzi was a criminal for a few days and did five years. Peyton Bragg killed four people the day he robbed the bank in Sallisaw with a Thompson sub-machine gun. Two of them were law officers. You don't allow a man like Peyton Bragg to go around with a Thompson sub-machine gun. That's the difference. You have to know,' Carl said, 'when it's all right to use your gun.'

All this to get the hard-headed bullrider to quit thinking every offender was a criminal you ought to shoot ... and every German POW a Kraut you could beat up if you wanted. And if you could.

Carl said, 'We'll stop at the Deep Fork camp on the way. I want to introduce you to Jurgen Schrenk.'

'I've met him.'

'No you haven't.'

In the bedroom of the Mayo suite, Carl and Louly were sitting up in bed talking, drinks on the night tables, an ashtray between them on the sheet that covered Carl to his waist while Louly was trying to keep it under her arms. Carl would use his foot to kick the sheet loose and Louly would have to hang on to it; she did a couple of times and after that let it go. Carl said, 'Why're you acting like you're so modest?' Louly said because she was, she was modest. Carl said, 'How can you be modest and work at Teddy's? Everywhere you turn you're looking at bare bazooms.' Louly said she never showed hers, even though they were way better than most everyone else's. Or unsnapped her teddy.

Carl said, 'You called yourself Kitty so it wouldn't be you working there, but you got to see all the monkey business going on.' He leaned over and she turned to kiss him. They loved to kiss each other, never in a rush. Their faces close he said, 'You're my little monkey,' the two grinning at each other.

She told him the war bond rally this afternoon went okay, on the steps of the federal courthouse. They had the Andrew Sisters doing "Any Bonds Today" piped over the PA system. 'And then Anita O'Day and Roy Eldridge did "Let Me Off Uptown" and "Thanks for the Boogie Ride" with an entire 17–piece band behind them. Anita brought me up to the mike with her and we sang that part, "I like riding in jalopies away from motorcycle coppies, I like riding just like you do aboard the Chattanooga choo-choo. So let me thank you gates, thank you for the boogie ride it really was great."'

Carl said, 'In your uniform.'

'Of course.'

'You snapped your fingers?'

'I had the moves,' Louly said, 'don't worry.'

Carl had to grin. He sure loved this marine.

She asked earlier if he wanted to go to the show, see *Lady in the Dark* with Ginger Rogers and Ray Milland, Louly reading from the ad in the paper, 'The thrilling story of a woman's secret loves based on the internationally famed stage success.' Carl said, 'What's it about?' Louly said the revealing of a woman's secret loves. He stared at her now. 'Yeah . . . ?' She wasn't that crazy about seeing it. They'd skip the show and have something to eat.

When he told her how he handled the Joe Tanzi business, Louly said, 'The new guy didn't understand what you were doing? I don't understand it either, how you can decide to let the guy go. What're you, a parole board?'

'They got mad 'cause they couldn't find the money and gave Joe twenty-five years.'

''Cause he hid it.'

'You think he should do another twenty?'

'What I think – what's that got to do with it? I don't have a say in it and you don't either.'

'But I said something, didn't I, whether I had a say or not. I said this isn't the guy we're looking for. I let him grow his cotton. You know what I wanted to ask him? What happened to his wife? The one left him when he robbed the bank. But I couldn't think of how to put it.'

The first thing they talked about in the hotel suite while they were taking off their clothes – then held up on that conversation for a while, until they had their highballs and cigarettes – was Carl introducing Gary to Jurgen.

Carl said Gary eyed the Kraut officer in his short pants sitting across his cot with his back against the wall, Jurgen showing no interest in Gary until Carl introduced him as a former rodeo bullrider from Kosse, Texas, not far from Waco. And Jurgen said, Kosse? Do you know Bob Wills? He's from there. Gary said no, but he's heard him enough on the radio.

Gary said Bob was great but he preferred the down home sound of his favorite, Roy Acuff. It got Jurgen sitting up, Jurgen saying Roy Acuff, it was Acuff who tuned his ear to hillbilly music. He'd started listening when he lived in Detroit. Saturday nights he'd tune in the Grand Ole Opry broadcasts.

Carl said once they got into the music, and started talking about Uncle Dave Macon, The Carter Family, Pee Wee King, the war between Gary and Jurgen was over. Jurgen hadn't yet heard of Eddie Arnold, a new singer, so Gary said he'd bring over some records. 'That's how it went,' Carl said. 'Toward the end Jurgen was asking Gary, "What's this about riding bulls?"'

'Guess who I saw in the lobby, when I got back from selling war bonds.'

They were in the bathroom now getting ready to go out, Louly plucking her eyebrows, Carl patting Aqua Velva on his face.

'Teddy Ritz. I forgot to tell you. He was talking to a couple of gangsters.'

'Why do you think they're gangsters?'

'They look like gangsters, and they were with Teddy.'

'You talk to him?'

'He looked over, but he wouldn't of recognized me in my uniform.'

'I'm surprised you didn't go up to him.'

'If he doesn't remember me, what's the point? But listen, Teddy wasn't checking in, the two hoods were checking out. With big suitcases they wouldn't let the bellboys get their hands on. But now I didn't see Teddy. The two guys were leaving the hotel.'

Carl said, 'You followed them.'

'To see if Teddy was outside. He was standing by a Packard, the high-priced one. The two guys put their grips in the trunk . . . The car was delivered by a hotel valet, he's standing there waiting for a tip. Teddy and the two guys got in, one of them driving, and took off. The valet still waiting for the tip they didn't give him. I went over and asked him, "You know where they're going?"'

'No beating around the bush,' Carl said.

'The valet said Okmulgee. I gave him a quarter.'

119

VIII

S hemane took a sip of her martini, placed it on the cocktail
table and picked up the Tulsa paper, the *World*.
NAZI CHIEF ESCAPES DEATH IN BOMB PLOT

Shemane said, 'Mom, the paper you're reading is three months
old.' The edition about Hitler escaping death and FDR accepting
the nomination for a fourth term; she laid it on the stack of
newspapers between them on the sofa.

Her mom was holding her martini and reading a Sunday
edition's Society page. On her lap and on the sofa she had the
World as far back as summer, even older ones in her room, Gladys
keeping up with the Tulsa money people, once her neighbors. She
didn't know how the paper got to Okmulgee, but there it was on
the front stoop every morning. Shemane watched Gladys in her
green velvet with the emerald necklace and rings, always her rings,
her veined hand reaching for the cigarette in the silver holder
resting in a silver ashtray.

'It s gone out.'

Shemane had on a nifty black jersey this evening with a scoop neck, no jewelry. She said, 'Let me have it,' flicked a silver lighter to get the joint going again, took a deep draw through the holder and held her breath saying, 'Mom? Here, take it.'

She had read about the attempt to assassinate Hitler, one of his guys, Goering – no, it was the naval guy, Doenitz, saying, 'by a clique of mad generals'. Jurgen knew about it, he said Hitler was crazy, not the generals, one of them being Field Marshal Rommel, Jurgen's all-time hero. She had read only a couple weeks ago Rommel had died of injuries received last July in France when his car was strafed by a Spitfire and went out of control. Jurgen said, 'He takes all that time to die of injuries? He was a war hero, loved by the German people. It's why they couldn't hang him.' His voice quiet then saying, 'They made him take poison.'

He said it during his last visit, the two of them on the sofa. She put her arm around him and brushed his hair from his forehead and kissed his cheek telling him she was so sorry, kissing and patting him and touching his hair.

Her mom thought Jurgen was a nice polite boy because he said yes ma'm and no ma'm. Shemane and her mom hardly ever talked about the war. Her mom would see a photo of Franklin Roosevelt in the paper and say Alvin called him a Communist Jew-lover. Gladys had grown up in Tulsa society, was snatched off a country club dance floor by Alvin Morrissey, who married her to get into Maple Ridge and make oil contacts. By the time Shemane was 12 she knew her dad was fooling around; she'd go through his things and find letters from girls, girls' names in his address book and rubbers in his billfold. She told Jurgen she told him just about everything because he liked to listen to her – that her dad had married Gladys because she was ditsy and loved all kinds of cocktails, loved to dance and drive to Hot Springs to gamble.

Shemane said, 'She misses her social life less and less. I'm thankful she knows enough to sedate herself. Mom can feel mellow whenever she wants.'

Shemane was surprised Jurgen had never tried reefer. He liked it, grinning and talking more, becoming less and less German each time he came, telling her how much he liked America and wanted to visit Detroit again after the war. He said you could ride the streetcar from the fairgrounds all the way downtown to the river for seven cents, and take the ferry to Canada for a nickel. He loved to read. He loved scotch whisky. He told Shemane he loved her and maybe he did, though a lot of guys had said they loved her. She told Jurgen she never tried to vamp her customers; she'd be herself, the nice polite girl-next-door-type, like this was the first time she was ever in bed naked with a guy and a little nervous but still anxious to please. 'I'd say, "Do you like it when I do this?" Very innocent. Like it honey, they loved all my tricks.' She told Jurgen about Teddy Ritz, an honest-to-God gangster who'd set her up with dates and take her back to his bed after, because she had been with rich guys, gentlemen, and Teddy would ask what they talked about and if she had learned anything he could use.

She asked Jurgen what being in North Africa had been like. He said, 'The best part? Being with Erwin Rommel, feeling his energy. It was exciting to watch him.' He thought about North Africa and said, 'Otherwise it was armor in the desert, all that metal painted the color of sand. Metal you didn't want to touch. And at night you froze to death.'

She could tell he liked the she way she was herself with him in bed, not using any of her tricky moves on him and made him wear a rubber. He asked her if it was necessary and she said, 'Trust me.' Making love, she would open her eyes and see him staring at her, very serious about it, and she would smile and see his face relax and everything would be all right. He never offered to pay her; she could tell it never entered his mind.

The phone rang, on the desk between the two front windows. 'Teddy,' her mom said. 'What do you bet?'

Shemane let the phone ring a few times before going over to pick it up. She said, 'Teddy?' and listened and said, 'You're the only one that calls.' Three times during the past few days. Her mom was smoking a cigarette now, watching Shemane, hearing her say, 'I read the paper, Teddy. We get two every day of the week and I read them, I keep up with the war and I haven't seen anything about—' Now she was listening again. Now she was saying, 'Yeah, but how do you know it's true?' He had been telling her about Warsaw, where his people were from originally – Teddy's grandfather with a store that sold musical instruments in the front half and the grandfather's brother repaired shoes in the back – telling her what the Germans had been doing to the Jews for almost ten years, awful things, Teddy learning about it from someone who was there and wrote to him. What Shemane couldn't understand, why he was telling her all this. She was saying now, 'You are? When?' Now she was listening. Now she was saying, 'Where are you?' sounding surprised.

Her mom picked up the cigarette holder and said, 'Sweetie, it's out again. How come it doesn't stay lit?'

Shemane returned to the sofa and sat down. She finished her martini before lighting the joint for her mom.

'Teddy's coming.'

'Here?'

'For a visit. He's in Tulsa. Every time he calls he tells me what the Germans are doing to the Jews.'

'I never did understand,' her mom said, 'what your father had against them.'

'Did you know any Jews?'

'I'm not sure, I must know *some*.'

'But Teddy never *visits*, you know, makes social calls. He goes somewhere, it's about business. You know what I think?'

'Did you know,' her mom said, 'Irving Berlin wrote "Any Bonds Today"? I'm sure he's Jewish.'

Shemane went back to the kitchen to pour another martini. The front doorbell rang, then again while she was adding olives and wondering who it was. Tony Antonelli or Carl Webster? Not Teddy, he'd still be in Tulsa or on his way. She hoped it might be Carl. It would be fun to try some of the old stuff on him. Shemane walked out to the living room in time to see her mom opening the front door to a soldier who was introducing himself, now looking past her into the house at Shemane coming to the sofa with her martini.

She heard him say, 'Shemane? How you doing? Remember me? PFC Larry Davidson. Remember that pecan farm across the river? You stopped and I came over to your car, that Lincoln Zephyr you were driving?' Yeah, Larry – she remembered him, his overseas cap cocked over one eye and the carbine slung over his shoulder. She remembered asking him if he was friends with any of the POWs and Larry saying, 'Are you nuts? Why would I want a Nazi for a friend?' It was the first time she had thought of those nice German boys working on farms around here as Nazis.

She was surprised Larry hadn't stopped by before this. He wasn't her first choice, but he was company and her mom seemed glad to see him, so she waved at him to come in.

'Larry, what're you drinking, hon?'

Teddy Ritz was making the trip in the comfort of his Packard touring car, 90,000 miles on it. Teddy, in his black chesterfield, had the back seat to himself.

His two hired hands were in front, the Tedesco brothers, Salvatore and Frank, known as Tutti and Frankie Bones. They both were wearing shirts and ties with their dark suits and felt hats straight on their heads, both with the brims snapped down on their eyes.

Teddy was telling them how the Germans were sending 6,000 Jews a day to Treblinka, the death camp only forty miles from Warsaw. 'The Krauts announce they're giving each person a loaf of bread for the trip. So these people starving to death think well, if they're feeding us they're not gonna kill us, right? Grasping at straws. They make the trip to the concentration camp and end up in the gas chamber screaming. Some the Krauts save to shoot and dump them in a pit. You imagine living there,' Teddy said, 'seeing this going on every day? Wondering when your time is coming?'

He watched the Tedesco brothers shake their heads. No, they couldn't imagine it. Frankie Bones, the one not driving, turned his head to say to Teddy, 'I don't think I ever heard of that many people getting knocked off on purpose at the same time. St Valentine's Day, how many was that, seven?'

What Teddy loved about the Tedesco brothers, before coming to Kansas City they were members of Abe Bernstein's Purple Gang in Detroit, during Prohibition. The Purples were a Jewish gang that hijacked liquor coming across the river from Canada and always shot the crew bringing it in. Al Capone tried to set up a base in Detroit and they told him, 'The river belongs to us'. They did do business with him, sold him booze and supplied him with gunmen, the guys Al meant when he said, 'Get me Detroit'.

Teddy asked the Tedesco brothers if they were ever in The Little Jewish Navy, the speedboat fleet operating on the Detroit River. They said no, they never went in for hauling liquor. Frankie Bones said, 'We take it over once it's been hauled.' They were strong-arm guys, enforcers going back twenty years you could hire today. Tell them what you wanted done, they agreed, you had a deal. They didn't need stories about Germans exterminating Jews to give them a reason; you offered five grand apiece to come down to Oklahoma and do a job.

Tutti and Frankie Bones. Teddy asked them, "You guys say you're Jewish?' They said absolutely. Teddy had never heard of anyone with an Italian name pretending to be Jewish for any reason. But they were, they were Jews on their mother's side, Diane Levine; she lived on Hastings and got to know Joe Tedesco from down the street.

Whatever they were, guinea or Jew, was okay with Teddy. They said they'd do the job.

The Packard turned off the main highway into Okmulgee and Teddy said, 'It's on the corner of Seventh, the Parkinson Hotel. We have three rooms under the name David E. Davis, who at one time cooked the best whiskey in the state of Missourah.'

Tutti said, 'Here's Seventh we're coming to.'

'You guys check in,' Teddy said. 'I'm gonna take the car and go see somebody.'

They moved the newspapers off the sofa so PFC Larry Davidson could sit between them while Shemane showed him how to hold the lighter over the bowl of the pipe as she drew on it. She said in a strangled voice, 'You see what I did?' handing him the pipe, a little briar she'd had forever, and held the light for him.

Now Larry was coughing and choking. Shemane's mom took the pipe and the lighter and drew herself a good hit while he choked. She told Shemane to give Larry the cigarette, you didn't get as big a jolt. Shemane said to him, 'Here, take a sip,' bringing his martini to his mouth. She was good at tending to men, seeing to their ease, soothing them, saying to Larry, 'That's it, baby, sip it. Another little sip. Now take a breath, ahhhh.'

'I'm surprised,' her mom said. 'I think we've introduced him to things he's never had before. Can you imagine,' her mom said, hugging Larry's arm against her green velvet frock, 'a big boy like Larry's never had a martini?'

'He's looking better,' Shamane said, touching his cheek.

'Baby, you feel all right?'

'Loosen his tie,' her mom said, 'and take his cap off.'

Teddy didn't arrive till an hour-and-a-half later. By then Larry had learned how to smoke a marijuana cigarette and was sipping his third martini straight up, with four olives, like Shemane's. Larry had never felt so at ease, so hip to the jive as he did with Shemane and her mom, the mom not looking that much older than her daughter and was filled out more. He said, 'You know you can tell things about a person by the kind of car they drive? And the color?'

Shemane said, 'Really?'

'I saw you in that green Lincoln Zephyr, I said to myself, there's a girl has seen the elephant, knows her way around. I bet she wouldn't mind going to Hot Springs some weekend.'

Shemane said, 'Hon, where're you from?'

'West Memphis, Arkansas.'

What Teddy heard coming in was Shemane saying, 'You poor thing.' The door wasn't all the way closed. Teddy pushed it open and was looking at the three of them on the sofa, Shemane holding the hand of the GI next to her, the guy lounged back in the cushions. Shemane looked this way and dropped the hand and jumped up glad to see him, always, from the time he took her out of that house and they got to know each other. Teddy smiled at her coming over. She always made him smile.

He kissed Shemane on the mouth, went over to the sofa to kiss her mom on the cheek and shake hands with PFC Larry Davidson, who didn't get up.

Teddy had no idea what the guy was doing here and didn't care.

Larry was grinning now, saying to Teddy, 'Are you one of the Ritz Brothers? I bet you get asked that a lot, huh?'

Teddy said to Shemane, 'Make me a drink, a manhattan,' and followed her to the kitchen. She started to tell about Larry, how he'd stopped by—

Teddy said, 'I don't care about Larry, anything you have to say. I want to meet this Kraut friend of yours, Jurgen.'

Shemane held up pouring the vermouth.

'You'll have to wait till he escapes.'

'When'll that be?'

'Who knows? He was just here.'

'If you can't get him to bust out, I'll have to visit him,' Teddy said. 'I want to see the camp anyway – take a look at these Krauts living like kings.'

'Why would they let you visit?'

'I'll say I'm a good friend of his.'

'I think you have to be related. Or you're a writer.'

'Yeah – I'll say I'm doing a story for the *Star*.' He saw Shemane roll her eyes and he said, 'They have tours?'

'Hon, it's a prison camp.' Shemane handed him his manhattan. Teddy raised it, took a sip and another, a good one. He said, 'You know who I bet could get me in?'

Shemane said, 'Carl Webster?'

IX

They were driving back to Okmulgee in the Chevy they'd been using, Carl at the wheel this time. Gary knew Teddy Ritz had called to see about getting in the POW camp, then called again to say he'd be staying at the Parkinson Hotel, but not under his own name. Gary asked Carl what name he was using. Carl said Teddy wouldn't tell him. Gary said then how do we find him? And Carl said, Teddy? You kidding?

Carl said Teddy wanted to visit the camp to ask Jurgen Schrenk why the Germans were trying to kill all the Jews.

Gary thought of asking, *Why were they?* but said, 'How's Teddy know about Jurgen?'

'Every time Jurgen escapes,' Carl said, 'he stays with Teddy's ex-girlfriend a few days, Shemane, one of Teddy's girls in Kansas City. So we'll hear what Jurgen has to say about the mass-murder of 300,000 Jews, all the ones that lived in Warsaw taken out and shot or sent to the gas chamber. I checked with McMahon, it's okay with him. He'd like to hear how a Kraut explains the death camps.'

Gary thought of saying, *I don't know what you're talking about.*

But now Carl was saying, 'McMahon wanted me to bring you along, you'll get to meet your first big-time gangster.'

Now he had something he could ask. 'If we know Teddy Ritz is breaking the law, why isn't he doing time?'

'On what charge?' Carl said. 'He has strong-arm guys with no brains do it for him. It's how you get to be big time in the business of crime, keep your hands clean.'

Now Gary was frowning, still confused.

'You respect this guy, what he does?'

Carl shook his head. 'I get a kick out of talking to him. Still, I'm gonna put him away, the time comes.'

Gary believed Carl should've told him before they left Tulsa, sat him down and laid out what was going on and what they'd be doing. They got to Okmulgee and angled in next to a Packard in front of the Parkinson Hotel, Carl saying the car was Teddy's; Louly had told him what to look for.

They went inside, Carl walked up to the desk and held up his star for the manager to see. The badge on her lapel said '*Maureen Whaler*' and under the name, '*Manager*'. She was 50 and sturdy in her gray suit. Carl said, 'Maureen, you have a guest wears a coat with a velvet collar, wears little glasses without frames, likes to chew gum and slicks his hair back with tonic? Maureen, he doesn't get each hair laying where it's supposed to, you see his scalp.'

'Mr Davis,' Maureen said. 'He has two men with him under his name.'

'How would you describe them?'

'I'd have to say, as gangsters.'

Carl said, 'You aren't saying it 'cause I'm a federal officer, are you?'

'I first saw them it's what I thought.'

'My wife said the same thing.'

'The two came in and said, "Davis", signed the card and took two of the rooms. Mr Davis didn't come in till two hours later. He said, "Davis", and took his key and went upstairs.'

Gary watched Carl pat the manager's hand on the counter and ask would she mind calling Mr Davis to tell him Deputy Marshal Carl Webster was waiting in the lobby. 'And tell him, please, I said I won't wait more than five minutes.' He gave her hand another pat.

Gary saw it, Carl making the woman feel good and the situation look easy. Gary watched her pick up the phone and ask for the room. She said, 'Mr Davis?' and repeated Carl's message. She said to Carl, 'He'll be right down.'

He was, too, slipping on his coat with the velvet collar as he came toward them saying, 'I knew you'd find me.'

Carl said, 'Teddy Ritz, I want you to meet my partner, Deputy Marshal Gary Marion.'

Teddy stuck out his hand not even looking at Gary and gave him a cold-fish handshake. Now he was saying, 'I could use a girl's name and wear a dress, you'd find me.'

Carl said, 'Where're the two guys with you, I want to meet them.'

'They'll be down. They're my bodyguards.'

'I hear they're gangsters.'

'Who told you that?'

'My wife. She saw you and the two guys at the Mayo'. Teddy was frowning. 'Louly,' Carl said. 'She worked for you she was Kitty.'

'The marine', Teddy said, 'That's who it was. I knew her but

131

I couldn't think of a name. Walked right by me. The short time she worked at the club the young rich guys that came in loved her. She had a list of reasons she used, why she couldn't go to a hotel with them. "I have to work". "I get caught I'll be fired". "I have to see my doctor about something". Or, "I fell off the roof this morning". She wanted to she could've made a pile of money.'

'Like Shemane,' Carl said.

'They were a lot alike,' Teddy said, 'they were both smart. The difference, Shemane didn't mind putting out for rich strangers, and Louly, Kitty as I knew her, said no and that was it. That broad, I can believe she's a marine.'

'You gonna see Shemane?'

'I already did. She said I'd have to wait for the Kraut to escape if I wanted to talk to him. So I called you, see if you could get me in the camp.'

Gary was having trouble again keeping up, Teddy talking about Carl's wife Louly, saying something about her falling off a roof.

Well, now the two guys Louly and the hotel manager said were gangsters came along, their hats pulled down, wearing suits and ties, a couple of dudes, but no coats. As they walked past one of them said to Teddy, 'We gonna be at the cigar counter.'

Carl watched them cross the lobby. He said to Teddy, 'What're they here for?'

'I told you, they're for my personal protection. They're brothers. The one that told me where they're going, that's Salvatore Tedesco. He's called Tutti.' Teddy said it with a straight face, though watching him Gary would've sworn he smiled, on and off.

Carl said, 'Tutti?' He did grin, making no attempt to hide it.

'The other one,' Teddy said, 'is Frank Tedesco.'

Carl was starting to grin, waiting.

'He's called Frankie Bones,' Teddy said, 'but don't ask me why.'

'He's skinny,' Carl said. 'That could be it.' He looked toward the two standing at the cigar counter and said, 'Hey,' and they both turned. Carl said, 'Come here, I want to ask you something.' They looked at Teddy.

Teddy motioned to them. 'It's okay, this guy's a friend of mine. He just wants to ask you a question.'

Carl waited as they approached and stopped a few strides away. He took a step toward them saying, 'Frank, why they call you Frankie Bones? You get the name when you were a skinny kid?'

The guy didn't answer but kept staring at him.

Gary watched Carl turn to the other one, Carl's hat and the guy's hat even, the two facing each other.

'And they call you Tutti, huh? What's Tutti short for; Tutti Frutti?'

Gary had an urge to get into this, move to the side and have an angle on the two concentrating on Carl, except Carl, what was he doing? Asking them where they got their nicknames. Yeah, but eye-to-eye, waiting to see if they wanted to make something out of it. Now he said, 'Teddy won't need you two inside the camp. There isn't anyone in there ever heard of him.'

'So what you could do,' Carl said, 'walk down the street to Deering's drugstore and get yourselves a Tutti Frutti ice cream cone.' He waited while they stared at him, Carl giving them time to say something if they wanted to. After a moment he said, 'My favorite's peach.' Cool, not once raising his voice, or taking his eyes off them. Gary had never seen anything like it.

Carl was saying to them now, 'So I won't see you two anymore, will I?' He waited for them to stare at him again, taking their time, before they turned and went out of the hotel.

'Fellas tried that hard eye on you,' Gary said.

'You're known as a tough guy,' Carl said, 'you have to act like one. We're gonna use Teddy's car, so you'll have the Chevy. I was thinking you keep an eye on the two mutts.

'Tutti and Frankie,' Gary said, glancing at Teddy who seemed patient listening to them.

Carl saying, 'But I don't want you to mix it up with them, okay? Or shoot them?'

Gary held back his grin and said with no expression, ''Less I have to,' starting to pick up on Carl's style.

'No, forget Tutti and Frankie. What I want you to do,' Carl said, 'is drive back to Tulsa and get Louly.'

Gary said, 'But I don't know your wife,' sounding alarmed.

'She won't hurt you,' Carl said. 'She slept in this morning but wants to see the camp.'

Larry Davidson was waiting by the door to the camp commander's office. As soon as he saw the marshal and Teddy Ritz coming along the hallway he opened the door to the office and held it for them, expecting Teddy Ritz to make some remark about last night.

No, what Teddy did was walk past him into the office and stick out his hand to Colonel Sellers standing behind his desk. He was looking at Carl as he said, 'I'm not about to shake his hand so he can put it away. I don't have your knack for acknowledging people I have no respect for. I've seen enough of Mr Ritz in newspapers and reading your book.' He said, 'PFC Larry Davidson,' looking at him standing by the door, 'will show you around if you want and take you to see Jurgen.'

That was it.

Larry said, 'If you all want to come this way,' led them outside and through the double main gates of the camp, each one in turn unlocked and opened to let them walk in, and closed and locked behind them. He heard Carl say to Teddy, 'I guess Wesley isn't in favor of treating a Kansas City gangster like a guest. He was in law enforcement twenty years before they gave him this camp to run.' Larry heard Teddy Ritz say, 'He thinks I'm a bum – tell him I'm a good citizen, I helped get a haberdasher elected to the bench who's about to become the next Vice President of the United States. Harry S. Truman.'

They walked into the street where the POWs lived, only a few outside watching them, Larry saying the first rows of barracks were for enlisted men, the next ones for noncoms, and the ones at the far end were for officers. Larry said, 'You see the three gun towers down there? The athletic field's on the other side of the fence, where they play soccer. Sunday there's a championship match, officers against noncoms.'

Larry told them these buildings they were passing now were mess halls, washrooms, latrines, library, canteen and the officer's club where they served three-two beer, and here was the rec hall, where they saw movies and put on plays and even musicals, in German.

Teddy said, "What's this place, a summer camp?' He turned to Larry saying, 'You passed out, you missed the show last night, Gladys doing a peek-a-boo strip, flashing her Charlies one at a time.'

Larry wanted to say, *Shemane's mom*? Jesus. But he'd just as soon not talk about last night. He said, 'Oh, and they play records on a juke box the camp got for them. You know what their favorite song is? Bing Crosby's "Don't Fence Me In". Honest to God.'

Carl said, 'Larry, we want to see Jurgen.'

Larry picked up the folding chair leaning against the wall, telling the guard on duty they'd need another one of these while the guard unlocked the door.

Carl said to Larry, 'You gonna pat him down?'

Larry said oh, and had Teddy unbutton his coat and raise his arms.

The overhead light came on as they entered the room.

Teddy said, 'You call this solitary?'

Jurgen was standing against the wall facing them, Jurgen in his shorts holding open a newspaper in the light from the small window above him, a heavy screen covering the pane of glass. He said, 'Carl,' and read from the paper, '"Barricaded Convicts Hold Four Guards As Hostages". Listen to this. "Twenty-five hardened convicts, revolting against being quartered with Nazi saboteurs, were barricaded with four prison guards tonight in the Atlanta federal penitentiary".' He said to Carl, 'Are there German saboteurs in America? I've never heard of any.'

Carl said, 'Jurgen, this is Teddy Ritz.'

'Ah, the white slaver,' Jurgen said smiling. 'I've heard all about you.'

Teddy said, 'You get a kick out of reading the news?'

Carl watched him bring a fold of newspaper from his inside coat pocket, a single page folded several times. Opening the sheet Teddy said, 'Tell me how you like this one,' and read – '"Hun General Bares Atrocity". That's the headline. The story goes on to say, "Major General Gilmar Mozer, former commandant at Lublin, admitted in a signed statement that hundreds of thousands of prisoners, including women and children, were killed at the notorious Majdanek concentration camp".' Teddy's eyes raised to Jurgen. 'The prisoners were all Jews.'

Jurgen said, 'Yes? What do you want me to say? I don't know anything about this. I haven't been to Poland in almost five years. Is that where you're from?'

'You guys kill me,' Teddy said. 'You're called Huns because you're barbarians, you're butchers, but you haven't been to Poland in five years. I wonder who it was murdered all those people at Majdanek.'

'SS,' Jurgen said. 'Gestapo. It's what they do.'

'You know any of them?'

'I have a comrade here who's SS.'

'What's he prefer, shoot the women and kids or stuff them in a gas chamber?'

'He's never done that. Otto was a tank commander in North Africa.'

'It's somebody else. You and Otto won't have anything to do with the murder of three million people.'

'Of course not.'

'But you won't do anything to stop it.'

'How can I?'

'Imagine being marched to a pit you helped dig,' Teddy said, 'knowing you're about to be shot in the back of the head and pushed into it. What do you think that would be like?'

Carl stepped in. He said, 'That's it,' and took Teddy by the arm to steer him out to the hall. In the doorway he looked back and said to Jurgen, 'When do you get out of here?'

'This is my final day.'

'Watch yourself,' Carl said.

X

The Tedesco brothers walked along Sixth Street in Okmulgee looking for a car to hot-wire and talking about Carl Webster, the guy Teddy called, 'the famous Oklahoma gunslinger'.

'You know what he was doing,' Frankie said. 'Get us to take a swing at him, we're brought up for assaulting a federal officer. I came close, you know it? I almost popped him in the mouth.'

'A guy you know packs,' Tutti said, 'you don't give him a reason to pull on you. We'll settle with Carl. I want the guy as bad as you do.'

They walked past cars angle parked at the curb one after another, they came to a '41 Pontiac and Frankie said, 'You like this one?'

'You want to get on the floor in there,' Tutti said, 'your legs hanging out on the street, all the farmers standing around watching you? Or you want to forget about a car and get something to eat?'

They came to the OK Café a few doors up Seventh, the place nearly empty at ten past eleven, and took a booth in front to look out at the street. 'I forgot it's Saturday,' Tutti said, 'why everybody's in town. They stand around waiting for something to watch.'

'We have to do it tomorrow?' Frankie said. 'What's the rush?'

'Sunday,' Tutti said, 'they're all in the camp, none of 'em off working.'

'They're all here today, aren't they?'

'Maurice is tied up, has to see his parole officer.'

'I never met him,' Frankie said. 'How do we know he won't choke?'

'He's a little smart-aleck colored boy, Teddy says he's a pro. Teddy tells Maurice to get us a gasoline truck so we can fill up our cars. Maurice comes back with a highway hauler, Texaco written across the tank. The time I met him Maurice had swiped more different kinds of vehicles than any car booster doing time at Jeff City. But you're right, what's the rush?'

'We put it off till the next Sunday,' Frankie said, 'we have time to look the place over. I said to Teddy, "Don't they have gun towers at this camp? Keep the Krauts from going over the fence?" He says it'll take 'em by surprise. I said to him, "You mean the guys in the gun towers are deaf? They won't hear the Thompsons going off?" He says they'll see a US army truck flying by the camp, the star insignia on the door. It confuses the guys in the towers. What's going on? That's one of ours. By the time they wake up we're gone. I asked him where're the trucks at. He said they're the ones take the Krauts to work during the week. Sunday, they'll be sitting in the motor pool not doing anything.'

'I agreed to do the job,' Frankie said, 'but I want to see the camp first, and not have to boost a car to do it.'

Tutti was watching the waitress over at the counter: watched her pick up a cigarette to take a drag and then set it on the edge of an ashtray. Now she was coming to their table, while Frank was saying, 'I see the Oklahoma gunslinger before tomorrow, he goes to the front of the line.'

Tutti spotted her name tag. He said, 'Norma, you behaving yourself?'

'I'm trying to,' Norma said. 'What can I get you fellas, just coffee or you're ready for lunch?'

'Breakfast,' Frankie said. 'Eggs over easy, bacon, fried potatoes, no grits.'

'Gee, I'm sorry,' Norma said, 'but we stop serving breakfast at eleven.'

'You don't have two eggs in the kitchen?'

'It's just how we do it,' Norma said. 'By eleven-thirty there won't be an empty table. But we have a special today, loin pork chops and 'scalloped potatoes. Or the pot roast looks good, with carrots and oven-brown potatoes?'

'I'll tell you what,' Tutti said. 'I'll have the pork chops and 'scalloped potatoes. My partner will have bacon and eggs over easy, fried potatoes but no grits. You need to bring the manager over? You can do that if you want.'

Norma smiled, not showing any kind of strain. She said, 'Let me see if I can sweet-talk the cook, okay?'

Tutti watched her walk back to the counter and pick up her cigarette. He said, 'I wouldn't mind checking Norma out. Except I want to see this Shemane. Teddy says she misses him so much she gets smashed every night.'

'Well, I sure need to see Carl again, get that taken care of. Before or after the job, I don't care.'

'You know what I think,' Tutti said. 'When this job's done, I don't see Teddy'll need Carl anymore and won't mind us taking him out. In other words, be patient. Wait and see can we get paid for it.'

Louly walked along the perimeter road outside the fence, looking at life in a POW camp: the rows of barracks across the yard where German prisoners were hanging up their wash. Gary Marion, staying close to her while Carl was with the colonel, said, 'Any of these Krauts yell at you and make remarks' – some were looking this way, some even waved – 'I'll see they answer for it.'

'They're guys,' Louly said. 'Don't worry about it.'

Getting Gary to talk on the ride down from Tulsa was like pulling teeth, until Louly said, 'Carl tells me you were a rodeo bullrider,' and that got him going. Yeah, he had some hair-raising rides when he was competing. He told Louly you had to wrap the bull rope around the hand you were holding on with good and tight.

'She comes loose on you, you're done.' He told her the bulls had to do their part; you got to draw one was mean and tricky to be in the money.

After that Gary didn't say much and Louly didn't know what to ask him. Where he was from in Texas and did he have a girlfriend . . . ?

Louly looked out at the yard hearing Gary say, 'The hell you looking at?' to the German coming toward them now. About five meters from the fence and smiling.

He said, 'You must be Gunnery Sgt Louise Webster. You still teaching marines to shoot straight?' He was wearing a uniform overcoat, open, and short pants.

'From the back seat of a Dauntless dive bomber,' Louly said, 'to shoot down any one-oh-nines get on their tail. I'm Louly, not

Louise, and if you know who I am you must be Jurgen the escape artist.'

Louly saw she was older than Jurgen by a few years. She had never thought of herself older than anyone. She watched him take a few steps toward them.

A voice through a bullhorn said, 'Back away from the fence.'

Jurgen did as he was told, looking up at the gun tower. He said to Louly, 'They say it twice, and that's all.'

'You tested them?'

'No, I saw a man shot.'

Gary got into it saying, 'He looked up at the gun tower and made what you'd call an obscene gesture.'

'He grabbed his crotch in a defiant way,' Jurgen said. 'I just found out Carl's married to a marine,' Jurgen smiling at her. 'What is it, seven years? He didn't say if you had children.'

'Carl said he didn't want to leave me a widow with a child to raise. In case somebody ever sneaked up behind him with a pistol. You must know Virgil, you worked at his pecan farm, didn't you? He told Carl not to worry about my ever being in want. I'd marry a couple of rich oilmen, one after another, and be fixed for life. Except I'd have to live in Maple Ridge with all the Republicans.'

As she said it they heard Jurgen's name called from out in the yard.

Jurgen turned and Louly looked through the fence to see Carl coming away from the main gate. He waved to her, then stopped and motioned Jurgen to come out to him, and now they were in conversation, Carl talking, Jurgen shaking his head. Jurgen talking and Carl, Louly would bet, looking him in the eye.

She said, 'They're serious,' and had to think about it because it surprised her.

Gary said, 'I know they're talking about *something*.'

The sauerkraut and ham for supper made Jurgen think of Carl explaining why they were called Krauts. He was already thinking of Carl in the yard this afternoon asking him to name the ones who killed Willi Martz.

Jurgen stood in front of the mess hall, waiting for Otto to finish supper and come out. Tell him Carl was getting tough, threatening in his own way, saying give up the names and they would see he was protected. Jurgen had to smile. He'd said, 'Send me to another camp?' and shook his head. 'You think they can't get to me? There are Nazi fanatics in all the camps.'

He saw Otto coming out, stopping to light a cigarette, Otto in his SS uniform this evening, silver medals and insignia on black. He walked past officers standing about talking and came to Jurgen.

'Are we looking for each other?'

'Carl Webster,' Jurgen said, 'the marshal—'

'I know who he is.'

'He wants to know who killed Willi Martz. I don't tell him, the FBI will interrogate me for days, wear me down.

Otto said, 'You're in a canoe on a furious river—'

'If I tell.'

'*Now*. Whether you tell or not. You're in the canoe and you don't have a paddle.'

Jurgen said, 'Well, I can always swim.'

'It's your only chance. The Committee is finally tired of you. They want to believe you're a spy for the Americans, so they're going to test you.' Otto motioned and they walked to a bench facing a flower garden, the blooms withering as the weather turned cold.

Jurgen said, 'Remember the red impatiens filling the bed? Except for the center where the white ones formed a swastika? It took them days to notice it. In their way they seem slow to catch on, but once they do they come after you.'

'I agree,' Otto said, 'but the Americans aren't our problem. I include myself because I've *sieg heiled* those cast-iron Nazis for the last time. The Committee says to me, "You're SS. See that you wear your uniform every evening." I can't tell them I feel like a toy soldier you wind up and it goosesteps. They tell me I have to give you the name of a comrade has stopped coming to their inspirational meetings, the ones that rave about the Führer like a broken record. The only reason I go, they open with a recording of "Der Blomberger Baden-Weiller Marsch", heavy, but always a favorite of mine. They want you to execute this disgrace to his uniform. Use a clothesline to string him up. Or your ingenuity, see if you can convince him he should commit suicide.'

'This is the test? If I refused—'

'One of their apes will strangle you. So, you swim?'

'Yes, I suppose—'

'Remember saying I should go with you sometime, your girl-friend will fix me up? I said if I ever went out with you it would be the time they'd quit acting like fools and shoot you? Now we're dead if we stay here.'

'When do you want to go?'

'Tonight,' Otto said. 'You understand, if we can escape, it won't be for a few days this time, but for life. I see this coming and I've been getting ready. I can put my hands on civilian clothes, suits made from uniforms, and I've looked at a way we can possibly get out – if you know how to hot-wire a car. You know whenever we have a film in the evening, the one who shows it leaves his truck behind the recreation hall.'

Jurgen said, 'I think I can start the truck.'

'Tonight they're showing *Louisiana Purchase* with Bob Hope and Vera Zorina.'

'I saw us walking out in our new suits,' Jurgen said, 'but driving out, *yes*, is the way to do it.'

'You drive and do the talking,' Otto said, 'with your American accent. I'm in the rear of the panel truck with cans of film.'

'It's perfect,' Jurgen said. 'We can't go under the fence now, the guard I gave all the souvenirs to has been transferred out.'

'Also,' Otto said, 'and this is most important. We write a letter, a statement, to your friend the marshal. We let him know it was the Committee who sent the apes to kill Willi Martz, and we list all their names. We say we have escaped, not to be free but to protect ourselves. For if we remain here, or we're transferred to another camp, it won't be long before we're dead. We both swear to the statement and sign it.'

Jurgen was nodding as Otto said, 'But how do we see that your friend Carl gets it?'

'That's what I'm wondering,' Jurgen said. 'But let's get ready. We only have a few hours.'

'Less than that,' Otto said, and looked at his wristwatch. 'We have to hurry.'

XI

They were behind the big recreation hall standing at the rear end of the panel truck, in the dark, waiting for *Louisiana Purchase* to finish, Jurgen in a black suit cut from an extra-large SS uniform, Otto Penzler wearing one tailored from basic Wermacht gray-green. The suits were from a wardrobe intended for a major escape the Committee was planning, all the way to Mexico.

The film cans in the panel's load space were *Salute to the Marines*, and *Dixie*, and *Commandos Strike at Dawn*, shown last week. Jurgen smiled, remembering the howls of laughter from the audience during the commando combat scenes. Now with *Louisiana Purchase* running, he would hear scattered laughter from the audience on Bob Hope's lines. When they cheered and whistled it meant Vera Zorina was on the screen in a dance number. *Dixie* was another Bob Hope/Dorothy Lamour movie.

'It's over,' Otto said. 'They're leaving.'

'I'll wait a few minutes,' Jurgen said, 'give the projectionist time to put the film back in the can and do whatever else he does.'

He closed the rear door on Otto, inside now curling himself among the film cans in his gray-green suit. They both wore white shirts and neckties, once tan, now dyed in strange shades of color, Otto's a dusty blue, Jurgen's deep red. He got in behind the wheel, came out from between barracks, waited for moviegoers to pass and turned onto the road that crossed the yard to the main gate.

The guard on duty wore a helmet liner and sidearm. He came through the walking gate next to the main one: came staring hard at Jurgen.

'Where's Lloyd?'

'A reel broke on Vera Zorina and almost caused a riot. You didn't hear the Krauts booing? It was right at the part it looks like the top of her costume is coming open. You know who I mean, Vera Zorina? Lloyd got the picture running again, but he's sending me to the movie theatre in town to get some splicing stuff. He wants to put all of Vera back in before we leave.'

'How come I didn't see you coming in with Lloyd?'

'I was in back. *Commandos Strike at Dawn* kept sliding against the rear door every time Lloyd hit the gas. He swore and I laughed, and he made me go back and sit on the can.'

'Listen,' Jurgen said, bringing a business envelope out of his inside coat pocket, 'I gotta hurry and get back, but before I forget, would you see this is delivered sometime tomorrow? It doesn't have to be first thing, so don't break your neck to get it to him. Long as you don't forget.'

The guard, a PFC, looked like a serious young guy. He held the envelope in both hands to read 'Colonel Wesley Sellers' and below the name, 'Commander, Camp Deep Fork'.

'It's about movies?'

'What's coming up,' Jurgen said. 'Have to get the Colonel's

okay.' He waited for the guard to open the double main gates and said, 'Much obliged,' on the way out.

They followed the back road that bridged the Deep Fork, barely a stream after hot summer months. Jurgen said to Otto in the rearview mirror, 'The man who owns this property is Carl Webster's father. He said I should see the river in the spring, at flood stage. He said it keeps the weevils from eating his pecan trees.'

The outside mirror showed the camp's tower lights against a black sky.

Once they were in farmland following a gravel road he told Otto to climb up front with him. Otto said, 'You keep making turns, following roads – do you know where you're going?' Otto the tank killer sounding a little nervous.

Jurgen said, 'The road of life, Otto, takes many turns,' Jurgen in a playful mood. 'As we wander the countryside looking for Okmulgee. I think what we'll have to do is take the first train out of here. We'll see if Shemane will pay for our fares, and give us a bit of spending money.'

They hadn't discussed this earlier, the idea of taking a train. Otto said, 'But we have this truck.'

'The projectionist comes out, looks around. "Where's my truck?" They go to the main gate and hear the guard's story, they know a POW took the truck. But we can't take it to Shemane's, so I thought we'd leave it somewhere in town.'

They came into Okmulgee from the west and moved along Sixth Street, Otto seeing most of the storefronts dark at ten o'clock. He said, 'There are no beer halls open? This doesn't look like our villages at home, does it?'

'It's what towns in the middle of America look like,' Jurgen said. 'All of them.'

*

The moment Shemane opened the door to Jurgen in his black suit and tie she knew this was the last time she'd see him. Still, she said, 'Well, look who's here. And you brought a friend.' She called, 'Mom?' and Gladys came over with her hand extended and held high, in case the German officer wanted to kiss her hand; he didn't, but seemed pleased to meet her. Gladys said they weren't expecting to entertain this evening but was delighted they'd dropped in. She took Otto by the arm to the kitchen asking what he'd like to drink, a martini?

Otto said, 'Really? Would you have bourbon?'

Shemane watched Jurgen turn off the lamps in the living room. He came over to her still at the front door and flicked the switch to turn off the porch light.

She said, 'I'll never see you again, will I?'

He looked through the glass pane in the door to see empty pavement in the streetlight.

'I'm going to tell you again,' Jurgen said, 'I'm in love with you. I don't want to leave, but have no choice if I want to stay alive.'

Shemane said, 'You're afraid they'll shoot you? They won't even know you're gone till the morning.'

'We stole a truck and left it in town.'

'You drove out of the camp? How?'

He said, 'Wait,' raising his hand, his fingers touching her lips. 'I don't have time to explain. But, please, if you and your mother will go up to your rooms and put on your night clothes, leave the lamp on by your bed—'

'How would they know it was you in the truck?'

'They don't. But when they tell Carl, and they will because he's still here, at his father's, Carl will think of me right away.'

It was almost 10:30.

*

Carl rang the bell at a quarter past eleven.

He turned to watch Gary Marion pull up behind the Chevy in the street light, Gary driving an olive-drab sedan borrowed from the POW camp motor pool. Now he was coming this way and Carl motioned him to go around back.

Shemane opened the door holding her silk wrap closed, her blonde hair hanging across her eye like Veronica Lake. He waited for her to turn on the porch light.

'Carl . . .?'

'I got you out of bed, didn't I?'

'I fell asleep reading Dawn Powell. I like her, but she uses an awful lot of words the way she writes.' Shemane yawned and said, 'Mom and I were up late last night.'

He waited for her to ask him in, but she didn't: he waited to hear what else she might say—

'What's going on?'

'Jurgen's out again.'

She said, 'He is?' sounding surprised. 'Are you sure?'

'A prisoner wearing a suit of clothes drove off in the truck that brings the movies. He told a story at the gate and was out.'

She said, 'You mean you think it might be Jurgen, or you want to believe it is.'

'I can see him doing it, talking his way out.'

Shemane kept hold of her wrap, her fist tight in the red silk, not anything like the other night, letting her jacket come open as she made their drinks. He stopped counting on Shemane asking him in. Yawning again, covering her mouth and saying excuse me. She did look beat.

Still, he hesitated.

She said, 'Are you looking for help or what?'

'Not if you haven't seen him.'

'Wouldn't I tell you if I did?' She said, 'Carl, I thought you and

I were on the same side when it comes to Jurgen. What do you want to do, come in and look around the house?'

'Not if you tell me he isn't here.'

She said, 'It's up to you, Carl,' Veronica Lake in the dim foyer. 'Do what you want.'

Carl stood with Gary by their cars, Gary saying he looked in the windows back there but didn't see anybody. 'If he isn't here, it must be some other POW broke out.'

'I want to be sure,' Carl said. 'Park down the street and keep your eyes on the house.'

'What am I expecting to happen?'

'He's in the house or he's on his way here, or it was somebody else who escaped.'

'But something tells you he's here, huh? Is it your instinct or your years of experience?'

Carl said, 'Gary, all we're doing is covering our butts. I'm going back to the camp. Watch the house – you see anyone go inside, drive over to police headquarters and call me at the camp. You see Shemane's Lincoln Zephyr drive off—' Carl paused.

'Yeah?'

'Follow it.'

They were in the sitting room now off Shemane's bedroom, bourbon, a bowl of ice and a pitcher of lemonade Gladys said for whoever wants a sour. It was time to straighten Jurgen out about leaving here on a train.

'I'd be glad to give you money for the fares,' Shemane said, 'but you know, cops, G-men, *somebody*'ll be watching the station and spot you. Your suits aren't bad considering where they came from, but they're . . . different. They catch the eye 'cause they look like they were in fashion about a hundred years ago.'

Otto was relaxed in an easy chair after a couple of bourbons and didn't seem to care when they would get moving again. Jurgen sipped his drink and seemed calm, less hurried than before.

When they were in the kitchen with the lights off they had watched Gary looking in the windows and trying the locked door. As soon as Carl left, Shemane came out to the kitchen and into Jurgen's arms to press against him and feel him holding her. 'He wanted me to invite him in. I said all right, if you don't believe me.' She said, 'He was a different guy this evening, not so sure of himself.'

Now in the upstairs sitting room Shemane said, 'You know I have a perfectly good automobile.'

Jurgen was shaking his head.

'Honey, I was thinking you could steal it and go wherever you want.'

He stopped shaking his head.

'But the best way to do it is if I drive.'

He said, 'No, I won't permit it.'

'Quit acting so German and listen, okay? I drive. Mom and I are in front and you two hoodlums are in back, under a blanket, we go through a town. If we're stopped, I say you forced us to come along, we're hostages. If that happens you're on your own. No one can say we went along for the ride. I was gonna say "for the fun of it," but I don't want to sound too sure of myself. Although I've been lucky my entire life. So I will say it, I'm going for the fun of it. And I'll bet my mom will too.'

Gladys raised her glass.

Otto said, 'How much lemonade do you put in—?'

Gladys said, 'Here, sugar,' and made him a bourbon sour.

Shemane said, 'But where're we going?'

Jurgen said, 'If you're serious—'

'Come on,' Shemane said, 'just tell me where you want to go.

'I was thinking,' Gladys said, 'remember how your dad used to sit in the mineral baths with a drink and then play blackjack all night?'

'That's not a bad idea', Shemane said.

'You know who runs the place? Owney Madden, he used to have the Cotton Club. I probably have friends there I haven't thought of in years.' She was about to say *Teddy loved to go for weekends*, but she was looking at Jurgen and caught herself.

Jurgen said, 'What is this place you're talking about?'

'Hot Springs,' Shemane said, 'over in Arkansas.'

After a while Gary U-turned the olive-drab Ford sedan to park on the other side of the street. Looking at the outside mirror now, his view was clear of trees and he could see the entire front of the house, even the light showing in an upstairs window. Once he adjusted the mirror he could look at it sitting low in the seat, comfortable, motor idling to keep the heater on, and that's what he did, he sat there staring at the house.

Was the Kraut in there or not?

He could find out easy enough; he imagined taking charge of the situation and saw himself on the porch ringing the bell. The door opens. Gary says, 'Excuse me, Sis,' and touches his hat as he walks in past her. She says, 'You can't come in my house.' In her nightgown you can see through. Gary says, 'Sweetheart'– he liked Sweetheart better than Sis – 'Sweetheart, you want to bring me the Kraut?' He opens his suitcoat and draws his .38. 'Or you want me to go get him?' Later on the newspaper reporters ask her, 'What was it he said to you when he came in?' That was how you worked it. Get a witness to tell what you said and what you did.

He saw the car appear, coming down the driveway past the house. It got him sitting up and now the house wasn't in the mirror. He started to crank the window down to adjust the mirror – realized all he had to do was open the door and twist his head to look in that direction. He saw the Lincoln Zephyr going away from him, getting smaller, gone by the time he got the army car turned around.

XII

S unday morning, Carl got back to his dad's while they were
having breakfast, Louly and Virgil, and Narcissa telling them
about a schoolgirl complexion. They looked up and Virgil said,
'You get him?'

Carl, at the stove pouring a cup of coffee, shook his head. He
heard Louly say, 'He got the phone call and flew out of the house.
All he said was Jurgen's out again. I yelled after him, "How do
they know it's Jurgen?" But he didn't hear me.' She said to him
now, 'Was it Jurgen?'

'Jurgen and an SS major named Otto Penzler. They went out
wearing suits and ties, in a truck that delivers movies.'

Louly said, 'Not planning on coming back this time.'

Narcissa had gone to the stove. She brought a plate of ham
and eggs to Carl, at the table now. 'I was telling them,' Narcissa
said, 'about this woman in an ad with a balloon coming out of
her mouth? It had on it what she was saying, like in comic
strips. Nice-looking woman. She saying, "Notice how many
men pick wives with lovely school-girl complexions?" My

question is, how do we notice it's what guys are looking for?'

'Or,' Virgil said, 'are they looking for schoolgirls?'

Louly beat Narcissa about to speak with, 'Who ID'd Jurgen and the other guy?' looking at Carl.

'They did it themselves. On the way out they left an envelope for the camp commander, but the letter was to me. They name who murdered Willi Martz and the ones who ordered them to do it. But we didn't see the letter until way later. They were having roll calls in all the barracks, see who was missing. But a lot of them playing games with us, not answering when their names were called, so we wouldn't get a true count. Jurgen didn't answer, but three others in his barracks didn't either. Wesley said, "We'll see how these smart guys like being confined to barracks a few days". He sent out guys to look for the truck and I left – went to Shemane's thinking it could've been Jurgen who got out. But she said, no, she hadn't seen him.'

Louly said, 'You took her word?'

'I left Gary to watch the house. Anybody comes, get to a phone and let me know. Shemane drives off in her Lincoln, follow her.' Carl looked at his watch. 'I like to think that's what Gary's doing and he can't stop to phone.'

Louly said, 'When did you read the letter?'

'It was sitting on Wesley's desk while we're waiting on the roll calls. I thought of going back to Shemane's—'

'To question her again?'

'To check on Gary.'

'Why didn't you search her house,' Louly said, 'while you were there? Why're you so protective of her? What did you say, "Have you seen Jurgen?" The whore says no, she hasn't? What'd you do, thank her, tip your hat?'

'I trust her,' Carl said. 'You ever meet her, make up your own mind. But you asked when did we read the letter. Wesley finally slit open the envelope, I think for something to do, looked at the sheet of paper, typewritten, and handed it to me. I started reading, I stopped and started over and read it out loud to Wesley and some of his officers there. Jurgen and Otto Penzler say they had to get out or the hardliners would kill them, and they listed the names. They swear these guys murdered Willi Martz, and that's the best they can do at this time. If we lock up the suspects till after the war, they'll come back from wherever they are and testify in court. Wesley was steamed up. He said, "I want those people out of my camp," the suspects, and meant right now. But this was a Bureau case from the beginning, I was only helping out the Provost Marshal's office.' Carl paused a moment. 'It's funny 'cause this afternoon I told Jurgen I'd throw him to the FBI he didn't start talking to me. I called their Tulsa office, Wesley standing there watching me, and spoke to the supervisory agent, Bob Grispino – we go deer hunting, the same guys every year. I told him we had Nazi homicide suspects for him. Grispo said he'd rather wear down an arrogant Nazi and get him to whine than shoot a 16–point buck from a mile away.'

'It's too bad,' Louly said, 'you and Jurgen were buddies. You could've put the FBI on him a long time ago.'

'I never thought of him as a buddy.'

Louly said, 'You didn't think about a lot of things.'

He should never've mentioned going to Shemane's.

'Honey,' Carl said, 'Wesley's already laid into me for fraternizing with the enemy, being lax in my investigation, and for bringing a gangster to speak to one of his prisoners.' Carl felt Louly watching him finish his coffee. 'Every word Wesley said was true and I apologized to him.' Carl laid his napkin on the table and got up. He said, 'If you all will excuse me,' heading for the door, 'I'm going to bed.'

He heard Louly say, 'Isn't my husband well-mannered?'

For the next few days he'd try not to mention Shemane.

'Anyway,' Narcissa said, 'you want a schoolgirl complexion so some guy will pick you? You have to wash your face with Palmolive soap.'

Maurice gathered up the Tedesco brothers in the '41 La Salle he stole when it was new and had kept it up. They put the cases with the sub-machine guns in the trunk and got in back, the two like gangster cutouts in their tight suits, hat brims snapped down on their eyes. Maurice had on a black overcoat with a furry black collar from some animal he hoped wasn't a cat. Maurice loved this car. He'd squirt cologne around the interior to keep it smelling nice. The two guineas were no sooner inside they were sniffing the air.

Heading west from Okmulgee Maurice was telling them about last night: going out to Deep Fork to look at the army trucks – in the motor pool outside the prison yard – and pick one still had the keys in it. See, what he'd meant to do, ease the truck out of there and hide it in the pecan trees down the road. But there was some kind of commotion going on, all the lights on in the buildings, soldiers running around, the motor pool busy, jeeps and trucks going out into the night . . .

Was Tutti interrupted him saying, 'You had a colored girl in here last night, didn't you?'

Frankie Bones said, 'I can smell her.'

'It's what I'm talking about,' Tutti said.

By now they were in the country, coming on to cars parked by a dinky white-frame church up ahead. Maurice eased off the road and could hear the congregation now belting out a hymn, a lively bunch of believers in there. He pulled in by the cars parked around the yard to wait for Teddy: Teddy's idea to meet here, see were there any last-minute questions, Teddy not wanting to be anywhere near guns going off. Maurice had a question: was the job still on? How were they supposed to shoot up the camp if they didn't have an army truck?

'What's wrong with using the La Salle?' Teddy said.

The four of them standing by his Packard while church service was going on.

'Chicago-style,' Teddy said. 'Drive past with the Thompsons blazing away, the slugs tearing the fence into bits of metal, like shrapnel you're throwing at the Krauts.'

What Maurice saw were gun towers shooting at his La Salle. He said, 'Boss, it cost you more to use my car.'

'I'll go two grand,' Teddy said. 'It'll be in the papers, but I want your estimate on the loss of life, how many Krauts these guys nailed. I'll be in Tulsa a few days – call me at the Mayo.'

Tutti gave Maurice a shove. 'Go wait in the car.' He had something for Teddy and said to him as Maurice walked off, 'Me and Bones want to make you a deal. We split five grand to take out Mr Carl Webster.'

Teddy was looking toward the church, people in there praising Jesus at the top of their lungs. He turned to Tutti.

'You want to become famous,' Teddy said. 'Make a name for yourself, the guys who shot the Hot Kid.'

'I got a name,' Tutti said. 'What do you say a grand each?'

'You kidding me?' Teddy said. 'You guys get the chance, you'll do him for nothing.'

Maurice drove the back road past pecan groves and oil wells, across the wooden bridge and through bare trees for a mile or so and stopped as he came to the cleared, bulldozed area: fifty yards of open ground to the fence running along the east side of the camp, the fence with barbed wire on it and gun towers, six of them, looking down at the yard.

The Tedesco brothers, in back fitting 100-round drums to their Thompsons, both looked up at the yard and the rows of barracks, Tutti saying, 'Where's everybody?'

There wasn't a soul in the yard or anywhere around, all the barracks' doors closed. Maurice said, 'Did all the Heinies escape on us or what?' Then he remembered Teddy saying something about a soccer match and told the Tedescos, 'I forgot, they all be down at the atha-letic field this afternoon.'

Except there wasn't any noise coming from down there, nobody yelling. Maurice looked at the tar-paper barracks again, row after row of them silent, like nobody was home.

Bones said, 'Go up to the field there, check it out.'

Maurice eased the La Salle out to open ground and turned right to follow the bare trace of a road that circled the camp, Maurice creeping his La Salle along, 15 miles an hour, and looking through the fence at every building on the way to where they were supposed to be playing, a gray sky over it, Maurice wanting to see some guys, some Heinies kicking a soccer ball at each other, even sitting in the stands would be all right.

It wasn't a bad day yet, but it didn't look good. Maurice cranked the wheel in reverse and got the car turned around.

One of the gangsters said, 'What're you doing?'

Maurice said to the rearview mirror, 'They pulling something on us. They knew we coming and they ready.'

'Who you talking about, the Krauts?'

'The soldiers, man. They got a hundred and fifty of 'em here. They in the barracks keeping the Heinies quiet. Waiting to see you gonna start it or not. Fire a burst, man, they come

'I was them,' Virgil said, 'I'd get over to Vian or Sallisaw fast as I could and head for the Cookson Hills. Best place in Oklahoma you want to hide out.'

Louly said, 'Shemane in her high heels camping? If Jurgen and this other guy, Otto, are in the car, I bet a dollar they're on their way to Arkansas.' She said to Carl, 'Where's Gary now?'

'At Shemane's. He's been waiting there since noon.'

'Why didn't he call you before this?'

'He's been hoping she comes home so he can give her the third degree. I told him if his car's in front of the house, park in town by the OK Café and I'll pick him up. I want to look around the house, maybe get an idea where they went.'

Louly said, 'So you'll be at Shemane's.'

'For a while,' Carl said. 'You want to come?'

XIII

Sunday, half past four in the afternoon, the Tedesco brothers were on their way to Shemane's: Tutti driving Maurice's La Salle, Bones in the back seat taking their Thompsons apart to fit in the cases. 'We get there,' Bones said, 'open the trunk and I'll throw 'em in.'

Tutti thought they ought to wait. See Teddy first, before he left for Tulsa. Bones said uh-unh, Shemane first, Teddy when they got around to him.

'I expected they'd chase after us,' Tutti said, 'the gun towers watching every move we made.'

'Teddy said they get tourists all the time,' Bones said, 'wanting to see what a POW camp looks like. Point out the Krauts to their kids've never seen any before.'

Tutti said, 'Tourists with a tommy gun sticking out the window?'

He didn't feel good about looking for Seminole Avenue, spending this time in Okmulgee, dragging out their stay while the colored boy Maurice was face down in that shallow creek, his hairy coat spread open, floating on the water. It was clear as day to Tutti they shouldn't ought to be here. But he wasn't gonna argue with Bones. When Bones didn't get his way he became ugly.

Tutti found Seminole, crept the La Salle at 10 miles an hour while he looked at house numbers, found the one Bones said was Shemane's and pulled up in front, two stories, big enough to be a boarding house. Tutti said, 'You ready?'

'I told you,' Bones said, 'open the goddamn trunk and I'll throw 'em in.'

Gary said, 'Why they doing that here?'

He stood a few feet away from the front window. The time he started to edge closer Carl took hold of his arm.

'They don't need machine guns,' Carl said, 'so this must be a social call. They might've known Shemane when she was Teddy's girlfriend.'

Gary looked at Carl. 'But isn't anybody home. They'll ring the bell a couple times and leave.' He said, 'Won't they?'

Carl kept his gaze on the Tedescos standing by a La Salle he hadn't seen before: the brothers talking, the heavy-set one, Tutti Frutti, nodding his head. Carl said to Gary, 'That's what you want to do? Be quiet as a mouse till they go away? You don't care to know what they want here?'

'If Teddy hired those guys,' Gary said, 'maybe he's meeting them here.'

'I called his hotel,' Carl said. 'He'd checked out, told them he had to be in Tulsa.'

Gary said, 'Leaving his girlfriend Shebang here by herself.'

'Shebang,' Carl said. 'You know she charged you two bills for all night? Stay here till they ring the bell, then go over and open the door.'

'You want me to open it ... Where're you?'

'I'm by the sofa.'

'I keep my hat on?'

Asking it since Carl wasn't wearing his.

'Yeah, leave it on.'

'Show my star?'

'They know who you are.'

'I ask what they want?'

'I'll start talking, you come back by the window, get an angle on them.' Carl turned his head to Gary. 'You broke in the back door, punched in one of the panes ... ?'

'That's all, and reached in to unlock the door.'

Carl watched the Tedescos coming toward the porch in their suits buttoned up, hat brims snapped down. He said, 'I have to run out to the kitchen.'

The doorbell rang.

It rang again before Gary stepped over to the door, opened it and stood looking at the Tedesco brothers looking at him. That was all they did, looked at each other, till Frankie Bones said, 'You remember this boy?'

The other one, Tutti, said, 'He's the squirt Teddy says was a bullrider.'

It caused Gary to think: Damn right, he strapped on to rodeo bulls that tried to kill him, and said to these two in their dress-up suits, 'I'm here investigating a Breaking and Entering. What do you fellas want here?'

They didn't answer. Both Tedescos were looking past Gary, so Gary turned enough to see Carl by the sofa across the room, not even looking this way, getting a cigarette from a pack on the cocktail table and lighting it, Carl with his hat on, his suitcoat hanging open.

Carl said, 'Step inside so my partner can close the door.' He watched them pause on the stoop, Bones giving an aside to Tutti. 'And you can tell me what you want here.' Now they came in looking around the living room up to the ceiling while they loosened their suitcoats, got them to hang open.

Bones said, 'Shemane upstairs?'

'She's resting,' Carl said, 'doesn't want to see anybody.'

'You hear him?' Bones said. 'She's resting.'

'Between tricks, that's what they do,' Tutti said, and looked at Gary by the window again saying, 'The squirt told us you're looking at a B and E. She upset about it? Bones's got something he wants to show her.'

'Yes, I do,' Bones said, grinning but trying not to.

'You stopped off and had a few,' Carl said, 'but you were here before that, weren't you? Stood on the porch and realized you better not ring the bell. She looks out, sees a couple of bozos from Detroit she won't open the door. So you went around back and busted in. But then you thought uh-oh, breaking in and entering the house wasn't a good idea. It wouldn't sit right with Shemane, and it could get you hard time at McAlester. You're thinking Shemane must've heard the glass break in the kitchen door and it scared her to death. You don't want to walk in on her and make a bad impression, so you decide to go somewhere and have a drink, come back and do it right this time. Ring the doorbell.'

Carl watched the two gunmen glance at each other, wanting to know what was going on here, Bones saying, 'Where'd he get all that?' And Tutti saying, 'He's the one's scared, he can't shut up.'

'Now I'm wondering what you had in mind for Shemane,' Carl said and waited while they stared at him, Carl believing they'd already decided how they'd play it. He said, 'You mutts gonna talk to me?' and glanced at Gary facing them from the front window, Gary's hands hanging free. 'Tutti Frutti and Mr Bones,' Carl said. 'We can hand 'em over on the B and E, lock 'em up till their hearing.'

Bones said, 'This boy never shuts up, does he?'

'You want to arrest us,' Tutti said, 'go ahead and try. Otherwise we're walking out.'

Carl said, 'Who's the car belong to?'

They didn't bother to answer, moving now in a lazy kind of way, turning to the door.

'The La Salle,' Carl said. 'With the machine guns in the trunk.'

That stopped them.

Carl watched them get ready and come around, drawing their revolvers, to see his .38 pointed at them. He took Bones first, shot him through the heart and shot Tutti high in the chest and shot him again. By the time Gary had pulled his gun the two were lying on the hardwood floor.

'Most times when you're late,' Carl said to him, 'you're dead. And you were late.'

Gary, frowning, said, 'I didn't know what you were doing, egging them on like that, getting them to pull their guns?'

This boy, Carl believed, was a long way from becoming a hot kid. He said to Gary, 'When you know it's gonna happen, you work it to happen when you want it to, while they're still getting around to it.'

Gary was nodding, but still frowning as he thought about it. He said, 'But how'd you know—' and stopped. The phone was ringing, on the desk by the front window.

Carl thanked God for this small blessing as he went over and picked up the phone. He said hello and waited, not hearing a sound. He said, 'I'm a friend of Shemane's. I'm watching the house while she and her mom – they saved up their gas stamps and are taking a motor trip.'

'Is that right?' It was Teddy Ritz. 'You got fired from the marshals and now you're a watchman?' He said, 'Listen, there's something I better tell you. Those two clowns from Detroit, they wanted me to pay 'em to take you out.'

'How much?'

'Five bills. I said, "You crazy? He's a friend of mine". But here's the thing, the way you antagonized them, I think they'd do it for nothing.'

'When did I antagonize them?'

'At the hotel, you called the one Tutti Frutti. Those guys, it doesn't take much to set 'em off. So watch yourself.'

'I appreciate your telling me,' Carl said. 'They're not your bodyguards anymore?'

'I let 'em go.'

'Where'd they get the La Salle?'

Teddy took a moment to say, 'A La Salle?'

'With machine guns in the trunk.'

'I have no idea what they're doing now,' Teddy said. 'I'm worried about Shemane. Where you think she went?'

Carl said, 'You tell her about Warsaw, what the Krauts are doing to the Jews?'

'Everything. She says it's only the SS and the Gestapo doing that.'

'So she knows all the Krauts aren't nice guys?'

'I convinced her.'

'Then how come she took off at four this morning with two Krauts in the Lincoln?'

'You're sure?'

'Everything points to it.'

'Jurgen. Who's the other one?'

'Otto the SS officer.'

'I'd like to meet him,' Teddy said. 'With a baseball bat.'

'He's Jurgen's buddy.'

'You put out a be-on-the-lookout-for?'

'This morning, an All-Points,' Carl said. 'It's Sunday . . . But a green Lincoln Zephy—'

'V-Twelve,' Teddy said, 'I bought her that car. No, it shouldn't be hard to spot.' He said, 'You think Shemane goes for this Kraut?'

Eight o'clock Sunday morning Shemane pulled into the Eastwood Court – 'Cool and Shady, Native stone cottages with radios,' and a 'popular-priced Café' – two miles east of Ft Smith on Highway 22. She said, 'Everybody up,' and told Jurgen and Otto and her mom, 'Here's where we hide out till tomorrow. We lost the tail, whoever that was in the army car, but you know he's put out a bulletin on us. Hot Springs is only 120 miles, but four hours creeping behind Sunday drivers. I think the chances are we'd get stopped.'

Jurgen said, 'Have you done this before?'

'I have friends,' Shemane said, 'this happens to all the time. I'm going to check us in. The rooms are two-fifty, do we need two or three?'

Shemane's mom, sleepy-eyed, said, 'Why pay for a room we won't use?' Otto the SS officer shrugged, half asleep or pretending, said something to Jurgen in German, and Jurgen, smiling, said that Otto's remark, essentially, was to agree to the arrangement.

'After I check us in,' Shemane said, 'I'm going to hide the car.'

*

Shemane drove part of a mile back to Ft Smith to NORM'S ALL-NITE SERVICE and had to pound on the glass door with the heel of one of her spectators to rouse the grease monkey who came with an awful breath. Shemane handed him a 20 dollar bill and said she'd like her car put in the garage on a hoist, all day. She said, 'If it needs the oil changed, go ahead. But if you tell one soul the car's here, or any cops that might come looking, I'll have you killed.' Shemane smiled and patted the grease monkey's cheek.

They'd brought gin and bourbon and what you mixed with them. Shemane put it all in her mom and Otto's room for their social gatherings and getting into heart-to-hearts. She and Jurgen could walk out any time they felt the need.

Shemane told Jurgen she loved him and liked him and was proud of him and she didn't even know him. And he didn't know her, what she thought about. Could he see her as a fugitive? That's why she couldn't count on him down the road, though it wasn't a bad idea. Jurgen said they'd talk on the phone and write letters. She said, 'Then I'll know where you are.' He said he trusted her, they could stay in close touch until the war was finished, and if they still had—

'The hots for each other,' Shemane said.

'I can come by your house—'

'If I don't drag you in and rip your clothes off we'll have a nice visit, do some catchin' up. Either way, I have to take care of my mom.' Her mom sitting on the arm of Otto's chair, the only good one in the room, giving him a sip of her martini and a drag off her cigarette, letting him put his nose to her skin to take in her scent – Otto the SS major who hadn't been this close to a woman since Benghazi.

*

Monday morning Shemane kissed Jurgen till his eyes opened, kissed him all over his face and rolled out of bed. She gave Jurgen the paper to look at car ads while she got dressed, slipping a black v-neck sweater on over her bra.

'What one would you love to have?'

'I don't see a Mercedes-Benz.'

'Look at Rollie Regal Motors, the guy wearing the toupee. He's got a low-mileage '41 Studebaker four-door with overdrive, radio and heater for fourteen hundred.'

'That's a lot of money.'

'Don't worry about it, Mom's loaded.'

Shemane walked to the dealership on Grand Avenue in her high heels that hurt like hell but were part of the show, once she was seated next to Rollie Regal's desk with her legs crossed. She told Rollie she'd buy that '41 Studebaker in a minute if it wasn't so dear. Rollie said he could offer her a '37 Studie for six-seventy-five. Shemane sighed, sitting with her coat open, and brought out a wad of bills from the v-neck of the black sweater, counted out seven hundred dollars on Rollie's desk and sat back.

'I have to keep enough to put down on this house trailer I want, since I'm gonna be living here a while, by myself. But I need a good car since I'll be driving to Hot Springs to entertain at private parties. I'm an exotic dancer.'

'Oh, is that right?' Rollie said. 'How exotic are you exactly?'

'I get bare naked,' Shemane said. 'Soon as I move into the trailer I can show you my act. If you want.'

Shemane and her mom said long goodbyes to their German fellas and watched them drive off in the '41 Studebaker that cost Shemane six bills and some vamping, but not much. She said to her mom, 'You think you'll see Otto again?'

'Not in a million years,' her mom said. 'How about Jurgie?'

'Maybe,' Shemane said.

She gave the grease monkey another twenty, got the car and drove back to the Eastwood Court, 'Cool & Shady,' to get her mom and the provisions and the few clothes they'd brought along, an outfit for Hot Springs. She got out of the Lincoln at the same time the sheriff's car turned into the court.

XIV

S hemane and her mom rode in the back seat of the US government Chevrolet, two polite FBI agents in front – a marshal trailing behind in the Lincoln Zephyr – everybody going back to Tulsa but without much conversation. Shemane was asked what she and her mother were doing in Ft Smith. Shemane said, 'We were on our way to Hot Springs, hon.' She said, 'You sure it's me you're looking for? All I do is dance bare naked.' It got the driver checking her out in the rearview mirror and the other agent turning to ask Shemane, 'You actually dance without a stitch of clothes on?'

'I have nothing to hide,' Shemane said.

Here was the Tulsa marshal Bob McMahon with police and FBI reports and newspapers on his desk – headlines screaming HUNS ESCAPE POW CAMP ! And NAZI LOVE NEST REVEALED – while Carl Webster stood at the map of America that covered a wall, Carl looking at the spread of country between Ft Smith, Arkansas, and Detroit, way up north.

McMahon said, 'You told the Okmulgee police the Tedesco brothers broke into the Morrissey house looking for Shemane, didn't find anybody home and came back later, when you and Gary Marion happened to be in the house. You accused them of having a contract to take out Shemane? How'd you know that?'

'It's how those scudders made their living.'

'They pulled on you and you shot them. I thought you got over wanting to use your weapon. Gary says you egged them on.'

'He kept talking about shooting outlaws,' Carl said. 'The time comes, all he does is watch. I tried to explain to Gary, when you know it's about to happen, you want to have something to say about it. What've you got him doing?'

'Court duty,' McMahon said, and moved on to Teddy Ritz. 'The Bureau's seeing him about the Tedesco brothers, find out why he brought them to Okmulgee with Thompsons.'

'They haven't figured that out?' Carl said. 'I want to ask Teddy why the two mutts shot that kid Maurice and took his car. I asked Tutti and Frankie Bones where they got the La Salle with machine guns in the trunk. That was when they drew on me.'

According to McMahon, Shemane planned to sue the paper for calling her home, where she took care of her mom, a 'Nazi Love Nest'. She told the agents she only saw Jurgen once, when he came to the back door hungry, asked if she could spare something to eat and she thought he was a vagrant. She never laid eyes on the other one, Penzler, before they showed his mugshot. And no, she did not drive them to Ft Smith. Shemane said she was taking her mom to Hot Springs for the baths, Gladys not having much pep lately. The agents thought the mother acted like she had a buzz on. Shemane said it was her mom's arteries hardening up on her.

With the newspapers all featuring the escape, McMahon wondered if the two had a chance of getting away.

'Jurgen'll want to go to Detroit,' Carl said. 'He told me his family has a lot of German friends there. Every Sunday they'd go to a rathskeller called the Dakota Inn and sing songs in German. Even knowing it's the first place I'll think of, I'm pretty sure he'll head for Detroit and hope to disappear.' Carl said, 'You know if agents checked the Ft Smith car lots? I like the idea of Shemane buying Jurgen a car.'

'Nobody saw the two guys anywhere in town,' McMahon said. 'Not even at the motor court where the women stayed the night. There wasn't one bit of evidence to place the escapees in Ft Smith, the report says, "So Agents did not make an exhaustive search at this time". You're the only one who thinks the two guys were with Shemane.'

'She's all they had,' Carl said. 'I'm gonna see her this afternoon, and I hope Teddy, before I take Louly to the station. Her leave's up tomorrow.'

'If the Bureau can't locate the Germans,' McMahon said, 'I'm betting they'll want you on the case. How would that sit with you?'

Carl shrugged and McMahon took it as an answer.

The meeting of Louly and Shemane took place in the hotel coffee shop. Shemane looked up from her club sandwich to see a redheaded woman marine approaching, coming to her table, and Shemane said, 'You're Carl Webster's wife, aren't you?'

'I'm Gunnery Sergeant Louly Webster. Yeah, Carl's my husband,' Louly said and touched her cheek. 'You've got some mayonnaise right here.' Shemane raised her napkin. Louly said, 'The other cheek,' and sat down with her.

'I've been reading about you and your love nest.'

'I've got a lawyer suing the paper.'

'You didn't entertain Jurgen at your house?'

'When you were working at Teddy's,' Shemane said, 'did you ever strip?'

Louly shook her head. 'Or take guys upstairs or meet them at hotels.'

'Any, my home wasn't a love nest,' Shemane said. 'I live there with my mom.'

'Carl thinks you drove Jurgen and Otto to Ft Smith.'

'He does, huh.'

'And bought them a car.'

'Is this Carl's idea, get us to talk girl-to-girl?'

'I teach aerial gunnery and Carl goes after fugitive felons. He doesn't put me up to doing any spying for him. I did meet Jurgen once, at the camp. We talked through the wire fence. I liked him right away. He has a good attitude and seems to maintain pretty well. The only thing Carl told me about you and Jurgen, you said you cook for him once in a while and you don't even know how to cook.' Louly smiled. 'He told me because it's funny, what you said. Carl has told FBI agents he believes Jurgen visited your home every time he escaped. Have your lawyer noodle that one. Or you never dreamed he was a German prisoner of war. I can't see you going to jail for being in love with a guy like Jurgen, even if he is a Kraut.'

She watched Shemane raise the cup to sip her tea, but there was no teapot on the table and the slight face Shemane made told Louly it was whiskey. Shemane touched her napkin to her mouth and looked at the trace of lipstick.

'What does Carl think will happen?'

'Carl lives by the marshal's motto – "Let no guilty man escape" – once he's convinced the man he wants is guilty. Carl has his own sense of right and wrong – and I'm starting to think the way he does, see the situation as a gray area where you can justify what you're doing or not doing, and tell yourself if it's okay.' Louly paused. 'Is that booze in your cup? I ask it as a marine who's been looking forward to a refreshment all afternoon.'

'Let me fix you up,' Shemane said. She caught the waitress's eye, raised her cup and nodded to include Louly.

Louly was thinking about Carl. She said, 'I'm never sure what Carl's gonna do, and I've been married to him seven years. I have a feeling he'd like to go after Jurgen, bring him back to testify at the trial. I'm talking about those six Nazis they're holding.'

'I read about them,' Shemane said. 'Charged with murdering one of their own guys.'

'The federal prosecutor,' Louly said, 'will need Jurgen and Otto's testimony to convict them, so there's a nationwide manhunt going on right now. What'll be interesting, if they ask Carl to get on their trail. He thinks they'll go to Detroit, at least at first. I said, "But if you know he'll go there, then he won't". Carl said Detroit's way bigger than Tulsa, two million people in a working-man's town. We know they turn out military vehicles, trucks, tanks, bombers, even boats, landing craft. Carl said he'd like to see all that activity in one place.'

'He wants to go after Jurgen,' Shemane said.

'He wants Jurgen and Otto to tell on the super Nazis, get them sent to Leavenworth to be hung by the neck. Carl said he'd vow to keep Jurgen safe till the war's over. Then you all can decide what you want to do.'

'He said that? Really?'

''Cause he thought I was jealous of you. He wanted to show he wasn't interested in you in that way. But he meant it, what he'd do.'

'Were you jealous?'

'Maybe a little. He seemed so protective of you and I got the wrong idea. The thing is, I came home on leave and in a week we had two good days together, beauties, but that's all, two days ... Though it wasn't bad at his dad's house this time, for once.'

'Boy, you two have something really good, don't you?'

'We like to argue, but we can turn it off when we want. I guess 'cause we're dyin' of love for each other.'

Shemane said, 'Wow.'

Carl walked in the coffee shop.

He saw Louly with Shemane, the redhead and the blonde looking like a couple of movie stars, talking, raising their teacups to have a sip, mmmmm, putting the cups down, talking again, Louly reaching over to pat Shemane's hand ...

By the time Carl saw Louly off and arrived at his dad's house it was coming on dark. They sat at the table by the windows across the back part of the kitchen, the chairs comfortable, with arms and pads on the seats; they could sniff Narcissa's cooking while they talked and sipped whiskey.

Carl said poor Louly'd be on the train all night and most of tomorrow, the Frisco to Memphis and the Southern line to Nashville, Chatanooga, down to Atlanta and over to the Marine Air Base at Cherry Point. 'Day after tomorrow the sweet girl's back to showing jarheads how to shoot down Zekes.'

Virgil said, 'Well, you seem contented for a change,' watching his boy sip on his bourbon. 'Remember putting off marrying that girl and I said you were crazy?'

Narcissa turned from the range. 'You said you'd be after Louly yourself if I didn't look so much like Dolores Del Rio. And you bet Dolores Del don't even know how to cook. The nicest thing your dad ever said to me.'

'Before she left,' Virgil said, 'Louly get over that snit she was in? I don't see she had a reason to be jealous of Shemane, Louly's better looking any day of the week.'

'Those newspaper pictures,' Narcissa said, 'don't do a thing for Shemane.'

Carl said, 'We're driving to the station, Louly says she's starting to understand how I think. How I can talk to a man escaped from prison, still has twenty years to serve, wish him luck with his cotton and walk away. Louly says, "Shemane's a traitor to our country 'cause she happened to fall for Jurgen?"'

'He was a hard worker,' Virgil said. 'All those Huns, they put their backs to it. They'd swat more pecans, fill more bags'n any people I ever hired.' He said, 'Tell me what happens to Shemane now.'

'I doubt she'll be convicted of giving comfort to Jurgen. She's got a good lawyer.'

'You have to testify if she's tried?'

'I'll tell what I know about the situation. Shemane understands, she knows I've already told the Feds about it. But I'm pretty sure she'll walk.'

'Now Teddy Ritz,' Virgil said, 'who came to town with sub-machine guns. You know why?'

'Tell me,' Carl said.

''Cause you invited him.'

Carl frowned at his dad. 'When'd I do that?'

'I'll tell you in a minute,' Virgil said. 'First, I want to hear what Teddy was doing with the machine guns.'

*

'Teddy said to me, "You haven't figured it out? The Tedescos wanted to drive by the camp, sweep the yard with the tommy guns and kill as many Krauts as they could". He says it was strictly their idea. He brought them as bodyguards since he planned to visit a Nazi camp.'

'Teddy being Jewish,' Virgil said.

'That's what he meant. But he says it was the Tedescos's idea to kill Germans.'

'What would they have against the Huns?'

'Teddy says they're Jews on their mother's side, from a Jewish mob in Detroit, the Purple Gang. Teddy says he happened to tell them, before they left Kansas City, what the Nazis were doing to the Jews in Poland and it must've worked them up and they brought the Thompsons, which Teddy says he didn't know anything about. All he wanted to do was talk to a Nazi, ask him why they hate Jews. I said, "But when they drove by the camp there wasn't anybody to shoot at. You know why?" Teddy says he wasn't there. I told him the POWs were confined to barracks for screwing up the roll call the night before, to throw off the count. This was after the two guys escaped. I said, "You didn't know why the yard was empty?" He said, "How could I? I told you, I wasn't there".'

'When did you talk to him?'

'This afternoon. I told him to expect the Feds before he checked out. Teddy puts on his innocent look – "Why? What did I do?" They'll throw the Tedescos at him till he's groggy. He'll start to defend the idea saying, "What's wrong with shooting Krauts? Isn't that what we're doing in the war?"' Carl said to his dad, 'But you're saying I invited him.'

'You got him pumped up. He should tell Shemane what the Huns are doing in Poland.'

'I meant call her on the phone.'

'But there's a whole camp of Huns right here. It must've got him thinking, uh?'

Carl said, 'He wants somebody put away's messing with him, he sends a guy with a gun. He wants a yard full of Germans put away, he brings Tutti and Frankie to do it, couple of mutts. One of them killed the colored kid and threw him in the river. They go to Shemane's, Gary opens the door . . . I'll have to talk to Gary, I see him, find out what he was thinking.'

Virgil said, 'You left out their breaking in, the first time they came to the house.'

'I'm gonna leave it out as much as I can.'

His dad took a moment, sipped his bourbon and said, 'It was Gary busted the pane.'

It surprised Carl. He looked at Narcissa.

Narcissa said, 'He's taking the Dale Carnegie course. Learn how to act like a grownup.'

Virgil said to his boy, 'You tend to make friends and influence people, Jurgen, Shemane, and get things going.'

Carl said, 'You're saying I started all this? By bringing Teddy here?'

'And you aren't through yet, are you? You going after Jurgen?'

'If they want me to. The first thing I'd do is find out what kind of car Shemane bought him.'

'You're stuck on that idea,' Virgil said. 'But if you work it, you'll come up with the car, won't you? You remember – you were 21 years old, you came home from shooting Emmett Long the bank robber through the heart. You remember what I told you?'

'Do I remember,' Carl said, 'I almost had it tattooed on my other arm. "God help us show-offs".'